**"Why are y**

"I wanted to make sure you got safely home," Troy explained.

"I mean earlier," Lakin said. "I know you were parked outside my parents' house. I saw your truck pull away when I walked outside. Why were you there?"

"I don't like that, after all these years, some guy shows up claiming to be your father and that he approached you right after someone broke in here."

"For food."

"You don't know that's really why they broke in. Because of the break-in and how shaken you were after Whitlaw came up to you, I wanted to keep an eye out. And I don't think I was the only one following you."

She didn't argue with him. And she didn't seem at all surprised either.

"You know someone's been following you," he surmised.

"I don't know for sure. I've never seen anyone. Did you get a look at this person?"

"When I tried, they drove off."

"And you sped off after them. You could have been hurt or worse, Troy. That was so dangerous."

"Yes, it was," he agreed. "This person following you is dangerous."

Dear Reader,

I hope you enjoy my contribution to the newest Colton continuity series, The Coltons of Alaska. I'm honored to be part of this series and had fun working with the talented authors who wrote the other books in it. I've always been fascinated with Alaska and loved the television series *Northern Exposure* and *Men in Trees* so much. With such an untamed setting, it was easy to come up with exciting scenarios in which to put my characters. I also enjoyed that they were high school sweethearts. I didn't have a high school sweetheart of my own, but I know so many people who fell in love in school and had long, happy marriages, like my in-laws. But even though Lakin Colton and Troy Amos are in love, their romance might not survive his pride, her stalker and the serial killer on the loose in Shelby, Alaska.

Make sure to catch all the books in this exciting series!

Happy Reading,

*Lisa Childs*

# THE UNKNOWN
# COLTON

## LISA CHILDS

**ROMANTIC SUSPENSE**

Special thanks and acknowledgment are given to Lisa Childs for her contribution to The Coltons of Alaska miniseries.

## Harlequin®
# ROMANTIC SUSPENSE™

Recycling programs for this product may not exist in your area.

ISBN-13: 978-1-335-47159-8

The Unknown Colton

Copyright © 2025 by Harlequin Enterprises ULC

Harlequin Enterprises ULC
22 Adelaide St. West, 41st Floor
Toronto, Ontario M5H 4E3, Canada
www.Harlequin.com

**Printed in Lithuania**

MIX
Paper | Supporting responsible forestry
FSC® C021394
www.fsc.org

*New York Times* and *USA TODAY* bestselling, award-winning author **Lisa Childs** has written more than eighty-five novels. Published in twenty countries, she's also appeared on the *Publishers Weekly*, Barnes & Noble and Nielsen Top 100 bestseller lists. Lisa writes contemporary romance, romantic suspense, and paranormal and women's fiction. She's a wife, mom, bonus mom, avid reader and less avid runner. Readers can reach her through Facebook or her website, lisachilds.com.

## Books by Lisa Childs

### Harlequin Romantic Suspense

#### The Coltons of Alaska

*The Unknown Colton*

#### Bachelor Bodyguards

*Close Quarters with the Bodyguard*
*Bodyguard Under Siege*
*Hostage Security*
*Personal Security*

#### Hotshot Heroes

*Hotshot Hero Under Fire*
*Hotshot Hero on the Edge*
*Hotshot Heroes Under Threat*
*Hotshot Hero in Disguise*
*Hotshot Hero for the Holidays*

#### The Coltons of Owl Creek

*Colton's Dangerous Cover*

Visit the Author Profile page
at Harlequin.com for more titles.

To the amazing and talented authors who I had the pleasure of working with on this Colton continuity: Justine Davis, Tara Taylor Quinn, Karen Whiddon, Beth Cornelison and Jennifer D. Bokal, as well as editor Caroline Timmings!

# *Prologue*

*Fifteen years ago...*

Once the bell rang for recess, ten-year-old Lakin Colton rushed through the open doors of the school and headed toward the swing set on the playground. Before she made it there, a small group of kids, three boys and two girls, formed a circle around her, trapping her. Then the taunts began.

"Nobody wants you!"

"Your parents dumped you at the grocery store like bad fish they didn't wanna keep."

"Like cans they were dropping off."

"You smell like fish."

"You're ugly."

Lakin closed her eyes, trying to hold back the tears that rushed up. It wasn't just what they were saying that made her want to cry. Raised voices terrified her, making her shake and sob, and sometimes she even threw up. They'd done this to her before. Maybe because they'd seen how she reacted, they were trying it again.

If Parker was here, these kids wouldn't be picking on her.

Parker was her older brother by two years and an adoption, but he'd just moved from elementary school to middle school. They had two older brothers, too, but Eli was in college and Mitchell would graduate from high school this year.

She had Colton cousins, too. Spence was in middle school with Parker, though. Kansas was the only other girl among Lakin's siblings and cousins, but she was tough. Usually she would be at school, but she was home sick today.

So Lakin was alone like the day she'd been left at the grocery store seven years ago. Although she didn't remember much about that time, about her life before, she hated being alone. Since Will and Sasha Colton adopted her, she rarely was.

If Kansas was here, they would meet up at the swings which was where Lakin had been heading. But she couldn't see over the kids skipping in a circle around her like they were playing ring-around-the-rosy.

"Nobody wants you."

"Nobody wants you."

"Shut up!"

She'd opened her mouth to say it, but the words didn't come from her. A boy broke up the circle, separating the kids and shoving them away from her.

"Stop being mean!" he said, his face scrunched up

with anger. But he was still the prettiest boy Lakin had ever seen.

Troy Amos. He had dark skin and really light green eyes. And he was bigger than the other kids even though he was just a few months older than she was. Maybe that was why they didn't pick on him even though his skin was darker than theirs, like hers was. He was half Black while she was probably half Inuit. But nobody really knew for sure what or who she was since she'd been so little when she'd been left at the grocery store.

"Stop picking on her," he said.

"What? Is she your girlfriend?" Billy Hoover asked. As usual, Billy's nose was running, and his red hair stood up all over his head.

"You like her!" one of the girls said. She was a pretty girl with blond hair and blue eyes, but that prettiness disappeared when she glared at Lakin.

"Yeah, I like her," Troy said. "She's nice. Everybody likes Lakin." Then he leaned closer to the blond girl, narrowed those pretty green eyes and added, "Nobody likes mean people."

The girl's bottom lip quivered, and tears filled her eyes. "I'm gonna tell on you."

"Go ahead," Troy said. "And I'll tell on you." He fixed his gaze on all the kids. "I'll tell on everybody this time. The next time you mess with Lakin, I'll do more than that. Me and my family and the Colton family will make you regret picking on her. So nobody better mess with Lakin again." There were even more Amoses than Coltons. Troy had four older siblings and two younger ones.

The boys scrambled away in fear while the one girl ran off crying. The other stayed for a second and mumbled, "Sorry, Lakin," before running off, too.

And Lakin was left alone with Troy Amos, her hero with the prettiest eyes. She decided right then, at ten years old, that she was going to marry him someday.

# *Chapter 1*

"Are you married yet?" Billy Hoover asked the minute Lakin walked through the door of Roasters, the local café in Shelby, Alaska.

Billy blocked her way to the queue. His red hair wasn't quite as messy, and his nose didn't chronically run anymore, but he was still the bully he'd been in elementary school.

However, Lakin had learned long ago to not let him or anyone else get to her. She'd even learned how to control her reaction to raised voices now. But instead of ignoring him, like she usually did, she pointed out, "I could ask you the same question, Billy."

Rumor had it that his wife had left him. Again.

His face flushed, and he glared at her before stomping out of the café like he'd stomped off the playground all those years ago.

While she moved to the end of the line of customers who also needed their morning fix of coffee, she was conflicted, feeling both a pang of regret for upsetting him and a surge of triumph that she didn't need anyone to rescue her anymore. She'd learned how to defend herself from bullies. Yet Billy's question bothered her—the hollowness she'd had before her adoption was back inside her, making her yearn for more. For marriage.

She loved Troy, and she knew he loved her. Although it had taken him a bit longer to realize it. Once he had, though, they'd become inseparable.

But he hadn't proposed to her yet. She didn't even have a promise ring to assure her that he planned to. They had talked about their future, about buying and running a business together like her father and her uncle.

Dad and Uncle Ryan had started RTA, Rough Terrain Adventures, when they moved from San Diego to Shelby twenty-eight years ago, after the family tragedy. They had retired a few years ago, though they were still a huge part of the business. Parker ran the company now, with Lakin helping out in the office. Their older cousin Spence was one of the most sought-after RTA tour guides.

While Lakin enjoyed working in the family business, she wanted to build something of her own. *No*, she thought to herself, she wanted something with Troy. She wanted to work with him every day and watch their business thrive…and hopefully someday a family of their own, too.

But Troy was insistent that to be successful, they needed to save before they made any large investments. Despite the fact that he made good money working on oil rigs, he didn't think he'd saved up enough yet. He was also helping out his younger siblings with college tuition and helping his widowed mother, too.

Because he was gone so much, sometimes Lakin didn't even feel like she had a boyfriend. She missed him and felt so lonely when he was away for months at a time. But Troy was coming home; she'd just received an email from him that he would be back in a week. That email was the first she had heard from him in much too long. While he spent months out on oil rigs, he usually managed to talk to her at least once a week via the radio on the rig or with a text or email that managed to get through despite poor internet and cellular reception.

Since she'd gone so long without being able to communicate with him, she wasn't sure if he was aware of what his older sister Hetty and Lakin's cousin Spence had recently endured.

Hetty had been shot. The wound hadn't been serious, but she and Spence could have died. The man trying to kill them had been a professional assassin hired to murder the guests that should have been on the tour Hetty and Spence were guiding. While they'd survived the ordeal, they had discovered the body of a woman who hadn't survived hers.

Lakin's heart ached with sympathy for the woman and her family while she also shivered a little with fear that there was still another killer out there. The assassin who'd attacked Hetty and Spence hadn't been responsible for that murder or for the murders of the other two female victims whose bodies had recently been discovered along Muskee Glacier Pass.

So who *was* responsible?

The authorities were working on it, some of them being Lakin's own family members. Her brother Eli and her cousin Kansas were on the case. She knew they would find and stop the killer; she just hoped it was soon. Because ever since those bodies had been found, she had a strange feeling she was being watched. Like a prickling on the skin between her shoulder blades or this chill that kept passing through her, raising goose bumps along her arms. She had the sensation now even though Billy Hoover had left.

Or had he? He could be outside watching her through the big windows that opened onto Main Street.

As the customer in front of her stepped aside to wait for a to-go cup, Lakin passed her bright blue Roaster's travel mug to the barista. She didn't have to tell her what she wanted; Lakin got the same thing every morning before heading into the RTA office: the Roasters house blend with a dollop of cream and a drop of caramel syrup. Hopefully the hot coffee would chase away the chill permeating Lakin.

When Fay, the barista, passed back her travel mug, Lakin smiled and dropped her money on the counter, enough to cover the coffee and a tip. She saw Fay so often that the young woman had become a friend. "Thank you."

"Thank you, Lakin, and hey…" Fay stepped closer to the oak counter and lowered her voice. "All anyone is talking about is those bodies showing up. Be careful out there."

Lakin wasn't the only one spooked about those murders. "You, too," she said. In addition to the three bodies that had been found, another woman was missing now, her picture all over the news. And then there was the Whaler, a local fishing legend who'd died in an accident that hadn't actually been an accident.

Shelby had always felt like such a safe place to live until recently. But it was still home. And she didn't want to live anywhere else.

What about Troy?

Did he really want the same things she did? She'd once thought he did, that they had a future together. But he was gone so much that she wasn't sure what he wanted anymore. Did he still want her?

That hollow ache of loneliness inside her intensified, and she flinched and closed her eyes. She opened them when she bumped into someone. "I'm sorry—"

"It's my fault," Eric Seller said with a grin.

The man was in his midthirties with a lean, athletic build. He was a frequent customer of RTA and flew up often from wherever he worked in Silicon Valley for day trips and weekend excursions. Clients had to book at least six months ahead to get a tour with RTA. Lakin worked in the office, not as a guide, but she still saw Eric Seller more often than she saw Troy.

"How are you doing, Lakin?"

He was a customer, a good one, so she didn't want to burden him with her fears about Shelby's safety. And, since he was a man, he was probably safe.

So she just smiled and lied, "I'm doing well. And you, Mr. Seller?"

"Eric, call me Eric," he said with a weary sigh. In every interaction they had, he pleaded with her to use his first name.

While she did with other clients, she felt odd doing it with him, like he wanted that familiarity a little too much. Like it meant more to him, like *she* meant more to him, than she should. And she didn't want to give him any encouragement. So instead of complying, she just smiled again.

He chuckled. "I don't know if you're shy or if you just don't like me," he said.

"I assure you it's neither," she said. "And I'm sorry you've felt that way. I guess I have been preoccupied because I've been very busy." Or at least she pretended to be whenever he came into the office. But instead of taking the hint and leaving her alone, he usually waited and messed with the personal items she kept on the reception desk. Like the framed pictures of her and Troy.

He glanced around the café. "Are you here with the boyfriend?"

She shook her head.

"Is he still just a boyfriend?" he asked. "Or has he finally proposed?"

Heat rushed to her face, but she was irritated more than embarrassed. Everyone seemed very interested in her love life today. Or maybe Seller had already been in the café and overheard what Billy said to her. Maybe he was just piling on like the kids used to do on the playground.

The question unsettled her, though. The press had given a name to the person responsible for the gruesome murders of those women: the Fiancée Killer. The bodies had all been staged with a fake engagement ring on a finger.

"Troy and I are both very busy," she said. Then she moved to step around him, but Seller stepped in front of her again. Blocking her from leaving, like Billy Hoover had blocked her from entering the café moments ago.

"Nobody should be too busy for love," Seller said, his head cocked to one side, as if he pitied her.

"And nobody is," Lakin replied with a smile. No matter how busy she and Troy were, she still loved him. She always would. She just wasn't sure how *he* felt now, especially when so much time had passed without hearing from him during his last stint on the oil rig.

Seller arched an eyebrow and smirked as if he didn't believe her. If he wasn't such a regular customer, she would have shut him down like she had

Billy Hoover. Instead she just smiled, sidestepped once again and walked away.

Maybe Seller was the one who'd been watching her earlier. Or perhaps he was watching her now as she left. Either way, she had that creepy sensation again, that chill racing down her spine.

*Someone* was watching her.

With a serial killer running around the Shelby area, murdering young women, the idea of being watched scared the hell out of Lakin. The Fiancée Killer had to be stalking his victims before he chose them, figuring out when they would be the most vulnerable. Once he chose them, he abducted them.

That was probably what happened to poor Dawn Ellis who'd been reported missing just a couple of days ago. Lakin hoped against hope that that wasn't the case this time, that Dawn would be found alive.

But until this murderer was caught, like Fay, the barista, had advised Lakin needed to be extremely vigilant…so that she didn't become the serial killer's next victim.

In his entire twenty-six years of living, Troy had never been as scared as he was five weeks ago when he fell off the platform on the oil rig and then felt nothing. One moment he'd been in excruciating pain from hitting the water and then nothing. Instant paralysis. He probably would have drowned, too, if not for his coworkers jumping in to save him.

If only he'd lost consciousness, too, but he'd been

all too aware of what he might be facing. He'd chosen to face it alone; he hadn't allowed anyone to contact his family or Lakin.

He would deal with whatever he had to deal with on his own. He hadn't wanted anyone to make sacrifices for him like he knew Lakin would, despite all the dreams she'd had since they were kids. So he'd spent weeks in the hospital waiting for news, for feeling, for anything but the panic that pressed down on him.

And then...

Feeling returned. At first it had been just tingling, but then that tingling had turned painful, like all his extremities had been asleep or frozen and were returning to wakefulness with a vengeance.

While Troy had been reluctant to get his hopes up, the doctors had been cautiously optimistic. The swelling that had caused the nerve damage in his spine had gone down, and the paralysis he'd experienced had proven not to be permanent. He still had some tingling in his hands and feet, and he couldn't move as fast or carry what he normally would've on the job. He might never recover enough to work on the oil rigs again. And he had to take it easy while the contusions to his back continued to heal or the swelling could return and cause paralysis again.

And next time, the doctors warned, the nerves might not recover as quickly as they had the first time. Or they might not recover at all. And he would be permanently paralyzed.

He moved slowly and stiffly as he pushed open the driver's door of his truck and stepped into the parking lot of Rough Terrain Adventures, the Colton family business. The main office was actually a large cabin with a metal roof and a big porch. An enormous garage sheltered their vehicles and equipment, and several cabins behind it housed family, like Lakin, or were rented to guests.

This place was usually his first stop when he came home. But this morning, he'd stopped to see a different Colton. Mitch Colton wasn't part of the family business—he owned and operated Shelby's local corporate law practice. Troy had asked for Mitch's advice with the situation with his employer, with the safety issues on his job. He wanted to address that situation as much for his coworkers as for himself. Mitch had promised he would take care of it.

But Mitch wasn't the Colton Troy really *needed* to see.

He missed Lakin so damn bad. He needed to feel the power of the wide smile that lit up her whole face and made her dark eyes glow. He needed to touch her silky dark hair and her soft skin. To kiss her sweet lips.

Every minute he was away from her, he ached for her. It had been even worse when he was lying in that hospital bed waiting for feeling to return, praying that it would. If it hadn't, he would have even less to offer her.

While she'd gone to college after high school and

had a bachelor's degree in business and accounting, he'd chosen to go straight to work to help support his younger siblings. Mom had already been working two jobs after Dad passed away. He'd been injured on an oil rig, too—but fatally. Mom hadn't wanted Troy's help, though. She had insisted that she had everything under control.

And she probably had. She'd always been strong and resilient. But Troy hadn't wanted her to keep working so hard. He would have felt guilty if he'd left her to manage on her own. As the fifth of seven kids, he used to feel a bit lost in the shuffle. Helping her and his younger siblings made him feel useful to her and his family in a way that he hadn't before.

Until he'd started helping his mom, the only person he'd really felt useful to was Lakin, as first her friend in elementary and middle school and then...

Then in high school, he'd realized that his sudden attraction to his best friend wasn't just unruly teenage hormones but that he really loved her. That he had probably always loved her.

Just like the Coltons had fallen for her when they first set eyes on the little girl their friends had been fostering. With her thick dark hair and big, deep dark eyes, she was physically beautiful, but there was also a spiritual beauty to Lakin. She had this sweetness and kindness about her that drew people to her. Some bad, like the old playground bullies who'd mistaken her kindness for weakness, but mostly good, like

Troy hoped he was. And yet he still worried that he wasn't good enough for her.

Wanting so badly to see her, he hastened his step as he started across the parking lot toward the office. But the faster he moved, the more he limped as those tight muscles in his back and legs cramped.

"Troy!"

He recognized that voice and turned to find his sister Hetty standing behind him. Then she started toward him, limping even worse than he probably was.

"What happened to you?" he asked, his voice gruff with emotion at seeing his tough sister hobbling. Hetty was only two years older than him, but she'd always seemed so much older and wiser and tougher to him than he would ever be.

"I was shot," she said, matter-of-fact.

He gasped like a bullet struck him along with her words. "What?"

"Exactly," she said. "How the hell don't you know? Where have you been?"

"Working."

"Bullshit," she said, her eyes narrowing with suspicion. They were the same green as his and their father's. "I saw you get out of the truck. You look like you've been shot, too."

He shook his head, then winced as a twinge went from the base of his skull down his spine. "I had an accident. That's all."

It was her turn to gasp. "Dammit, Troy. Do you

know how Mom would feel if we lost you like we lost Dad?"

He knew. That was another reason he hadn't wanted to contact anyone after the accident. Not until he knew how much—if at all—he was going to recover.

Hetty answered her own question. "It would kill her."

"I'm not the only one with a dangerous job. And you're the daredevil in the family," he reminded the pilot. "How the hell did you get shot?"

She sighed. "It's…a long story. There's been a lot going on since you've been gone."

"But you're okay now?" he asked, his heart beating fast with concern.

Hetty smiled, and her eyes lit up with a happiness he hadn't seen in her since their dad died. "I've never been better. I'm in love."

"Really?" Troy asked. She'd always been so tough and independent. "Who's the lucky guy?"

"Spence Colton."

Shocked at her declaration, Troy whistled between his teeth. "Did hell freeze over?" For years, she'd fought with and complained about the RTA tour guide, probably mostly because Spence had been so popular, especially with their female guests.

She laughed. "Well, getting seriously hurt puts things in perspective," she said, then narrowed her eyes again. "Doesn't it?"

Troy nodded. He just wasn't sure how to handle

that perspective, or how to even move forward with a future that was still so uncertain. Maybe he shouldn't have come to RTA or even home to Shelby. Maybe he should just stay away from Lakin.

She had so many dreams. She wanted a business of her own, one they could build and manage together. When he'd finally emailed her, he realized she messaged him much more frequently than he did her.

But when he was on the rig, he worked such long hours that he fell into bed exhausted at the end of a shift. In her emails she'd told him about the old Shelby Hotel going up for auction. Unfortunately the date of the auction had already passed. Not that they would have had enough money to buy it and invest in the extensive remodeling the two-story building needed to make it operational again. Those extensive renovations would also require a lot of manpower.

And right now, Troy didn't have the money or the physical ability to turn the hotel into the business Lakin wanted it to be. After so many weeks of not talking to her, he wasn't sure that he even had Lakin anymore. After so much time with no contact from him, maybe she'd realized she didn't need him anymore, that she didn't want him anymore. But Lakin, being Lakin, wouldn't break up via email or text. She would wait until he was home to do it in person.

"Let's talk," Troy said to his sister. "I want to hear about everything that happened to you. Everything that happened while I was gone."

She glanced toward the office. "You don't want to talk to Lakin first?"

He wanted to do more than talk to his longtime love. His body ached for hers; he'd been gone too long. But then his body just ached a lot now. And he was scared of what the future might hold. How angry was she with him for being out of touch for so long? She would also be so upset that they'd missed out on the opportunity to buy the old hotel.

Unfortunately, they wouldn't have been able to even if he'd been in communication with her. He was helping his mother with his brother's college tuition; he hadn't managed to save enough yet for the future Lakin envisioned for them. He needed to work a couple more years on the rigs to get enough for them to open and operate something like a hotel, especially one that needed as many renovations as the old Shelby Hotel.

What if he wasn't able to physically work on the rigs anymore? He might never be able to help make Lakin's dreams come true.

And then he wouldn't be the partner she needed and deserved.

"Lakin's working," Troy reminded his sister. "Instead of interrupting something, I should wait until she's done for the day."

Hetty's brow furrowed beneath a lock of her thick black hair. "You know she's going to be thrilled to see you. She always is."

True. Every time he came home after months spent

away from her, it felt like they were on a vacation or a honeymoon. Lakin's entire face would light up with a smile and she'd run into his arms, arms that longed to hold her. She would take some personal days off work, and they would spend as much time as they could in bed or on the couch or in a tent in the woods, just being together in every way. Making up for lost time was what they called it.

The weeks Troy had spent in a hospital bed, waiting for his back to heal, had been lost time. While Mitch figured Troy might have a case against the oil company, Troy wasn't as convinced. When his dad died, there had been no payout because that would have been an admission of poor safety protocols in the workplace. And the oil company was not about to admit to violating safety rules. The lawyer his mother had been able to afford hadn't found enough evidence to convince a civil court judge to make the company pay them anything either. Troy wasn't sure he had enough evidence either.

And if he didn't, there was no making up for what he'd lost, money, work and maybe even relationship-wise.


The photograph was more than twenty years old, so it was frayed on the edges and the colors were so faded that it was nearly black and white. Yet the man holding it knew exactly who the people in that picture were.

One of them was him, but a younger, more muscular version with thick hair and a cockiness in the way he stood that he didn't feel anymore. He knew more now than he had then, so much more. He wouldn't wind up where he had before; he was smarter now.

He drew in a deep breath and focused on the other people in the picture he held in the palm of his hand. He'd been studying it for a while as he sat in the battered pickup truck he'd *borrowed* a few weeks ago. He knew the other people in that old photograph, too, the dark-haired woman and the dark-haired toddler she held in her arms.

That toddler had grown up and looked like the woman now, almost eerily so, like she was her ghost. The first time he saw her in Shelby, he thought he really had seen a ghost.

But she was real, the young woman. He'd finally found her, and he'd spent the past couple of weeks following her around from the coffee shop she stopped at every morning to her job at the adventure tour company. She lived there, too, in one of the small cabins on the property.

He knew everywhere she went and everything she did now. He'd been watching her to learn her routine and to figure out what he was going to do about her.

Or get out of her.

Because there was a reason that he'd tracked down that young woman. There was some unfinished business between them. And it was well past time that he finished it, and maybe her as well.

## *Chapter 2*

When Troy's truck pulled into the parking lot of RTA, Lakin noticed immediately. Even if she hadn't seen the rusted old pickup through the office's big windows, she would have known. She'd always been able to sense when he was close; it was as if her whole body tingled with awareness of him. Before she could disengage from the client talking her ear off on the telephone, he was gone again.

He'd been heading toward the office when Hetty caught up with him. She knew, of course, that Hetty was still recovering from her gunshot wound. But was Troy limping, too?

Maybe he'd just been stiff from the long trip from the offshore oil rigs. Of course he wouldn't have been shot like Hetty. Nothing bad could have happened to him, or someone would have notified her or at least his family.

Troy and Hetty probably had a lot to catch up on, and that was why he'd left. But without even stopping by the office to give her a quick kiss? If she hadn't been on the phone with a client, she would have run out to greet him like she always did. She'd missed him so much when he was gone that she couldn't wait to see his handsome face again, to kiss him, to hug him.

And he hadn't even stuck his head in the office to smile at her before leaving again?

Maybe he'd found out what she'd done, and he was mad at her.

But only a few people besides her knew. And her dad wouldn't share her secret until she started sharing it herself. He understood her reasons for wanting to keep it quiet until she was ready to announce it to other members of their family. They might be the hardest to tell. And Troy...

Would he be happy about it?

Unfortunately she doubted it. He was so determined to wait, and not just when it came to starting their business together. He seemed determined to wait for them to start their life together as well. Marriage. A family. All the things they'd been talking about since they started dating in high school and he'd finally realized what she'd known all along: they were soulmates. But now, it seemed like he wasn't in any hurry to give her the commitment she wanted.

Maybe she was just letting Billy Hoover and Eric Seller's comments get to her. Instead of understanding Troy's reasons for working on the oil rigs, she was beginning to think they were just excuses to put off their future. Maybe she was just getting sick of waiting for Troy. And sick of missing him.

She was so sick of it that she felt nauseous. Or was that nerves churning her stomach because she was worried that he was going to be angry with her? Not that he really had any reason to be, not after going so long with so little communication. If anyone should be angry, it should be her.

If only she didn't love him so damn much…

He was a good guy. So protective and loyal and caring. All he wanted to do was help the people he loved.

But was she still one of those people?

"You don't look so good," Parker said the minute he stepped out of his private office. The administrative building was a big old cabin and felt more like a home than a workspace. The floor was polished concrete, and there was wood everywhere and big, thickly cushioned leather furniture where guests and family often lounged while waiting for a tour to start.

Parker hadn't even walked up to her desk before he made his pronouncement. He was perceptive as ever. He'd taken RTA to the next level, rebranding the company after their father and uncle retired and making it even more successful than it had been. Lakin loved working with him and had learned so much from him that she had the skills to run her own business now. She just needed help—the partnership she'd dreamed of having, in every aspect of their lives, with Troy.

"Lakin?" Parker asked, his voice deep with concern. "Are you okay?"

She nodded, then grimaced at the tension headache forming behind her eyes. That, coupled with some nausea, made her wonder if she had picked up a virus.

She was pretty sure it was just stress. If she admitted that to her brother, though, he would want to fix it. Her three older brothers had always been super protective of her, just like Troy; that was probably the only reason they'd accepted him as her boyfriend, because he was so much like them.

Maybe she should have been offended that they didn't think she could protect herself, but like Troy, she loved them so damn much that she could never be angry with them. They were the best big brothers she could ever imagine anyone having.

"I'm fine," she tried to assure him. "Just probably not sleeping well right now."

Because of what she'd done…and that feeling she'd been having that someone was watching her. But *who*…and why?

"I don't think anyone is sleeping well right now," Parker said. "Not with some maniac out there abducting and killing women. Are you sure you shouldn't be staying with Dad and Mom instead of in that cabin all by yourself?"

"I'm fine," she repeated. "I lock my doors and windows and keep an eye out." Even though she'd been super careful, she hadn't figured out who was watching her. Maybe nobody was, and she was just being paranoid because of the killer.

"That's good," Parker said. "And I'm sure Eli will find the bastard soon and put him behind bars for the rest of his life."

"I hope he finds Dawn Ellis soon," Lakin said, "and alive and well." She'd never met the missing young woman, but she was worried about her.

Parker nodded. "Yeah, me, too." He stepped closer to the reception desk and narrowed his eyes as he studied her face. He must have noticed the dark circles under her eyes. "Go home and get some rest. I'll handle the office for the rest of the day."

She smiled. "It's almost quitting time."

He chuckled. "Yeah. That's why I can handle it on my own."

He was obviously on his way out, so she shouldn't take him up on his offer. But she was feeling too sick, with nerves and a bad stomach and a headache, to stay. So she grabbed her bag and headed toward the door.

"Hey, you didn't drive here?" Parker asked. He must have looked out at the parking lot and noticed her SUV wasn't there.

"No. I left my vehicle at the cabin."

"Let me lock up and walk you to your place," Parker said.

She laughed and shook her head. "You're not getting off desk duty that easily," she said. "We're getting a delivery with the toner I need for the printer, and someone has to be here for them to leave it."

Parker groaned.

"You just have to—"

"I know how to sign for a package," he told her. "I don't like you walking by yourself."

"I walk by myself all the time," she said. "I'll be fine."

"Lakin—"

"I know," she said before he could bring up the serial killer again. "I'm always aware of my surroundings, and I'm very cautious. I'll be fine."

Parker still looked worried, but he nodded begrudgingly.

She understood his concern. Her own worries didn't end when she stepped outside into the cool afternoon air.

What would Parker do when she wasn't here to help him? She felt a twinge of guilt that she wanted to leave. RTA was family, and she felt like she was betraying them. But if she had help with her new venture, she would be able to train her replacement. If she had Troy...

She needed to talk to him. Really talk. Of course, usually after these long stretches apart, talking was the last thing they did. First she ran to him and leaped into his arms, then wrapped hers around his neck and pulled his head down for her kisses. Just thinking about his mouth against hers, his strong arms holding her, had her flesh tingling and heating up.

Her legs weakened a bit, and she nearly stumbled as she walked toward her cabin. It was farthest from the office and close to the woods. She'd chosen it because she liked the solitude of being farther away from the other cabins, especially when Troy was home from the oil rigs.

But now...

She shivered at the isolation as she passed the last unoccupied cabin. She'd parked her SUV at her cabin when she came back from Roasters that morning, but she wished now that she'd parked at the office.

No. She spent entirely too much time at her desk and liked to walk outside as much as she could, whenever she could. While she liked to be outside for the fresh air, she wasn't into the extreme outdoor adventures her family business offered. She preferred her cabin and her soft bed to a tent and a sleeping bag. And the farthest she liked to hike was to her cabin from the office.

That was a moot point now. After what she'd done, she wasn't going to get much time outside, especially if she couldn't convince Troy to help her with her new venture. Maybe she shouldn't be worried about him helping her; maybe she should be worried that he might break up with her over making such a big decision without discussing it with him.

But she'd tried.

He was the one who was out of touch for weeks, sometimes months, at a time. And that was getting old.

Especially now with a killer on the loose. Being alone so much was unnerving. Maybe Parker was right; maybe she should stay with Mom and Dad until the killer was caught.

Eli would catch him. Her big brother was the best agent with the Alaska Bureau of Investigations. And this case was personal to him. She knew why; it reminded him of how he and Dad had found Aunt Caroline all those years ago. Dressed up with a fake engagement ring on her finger, the young model had only been seventeen. She hadn't been anyone's fiancée, but an obsessed fan had thought she was his. He'd taken her life, her parents' lives and his own. And Dad and Eli, when he was just six or seven years old, had found their bodies.

That was why Dad and Uncle Ryan had moved from San Diego and started over in Shelby, where no one knew what had happened. For nearly thirty years, there had been no reminders of that horrible time.

But now…

It was as if that dead killer was starting over, too.

Lakin wondered if Eli was having nightmares again like he occasionally had as a kid. His nightmares had helped her feel better about the ones she had, like she wasn't so weak and messed up. Because Eli definitely wasn't. She wasn't even sure he remembered having them, but he and their father had been extra comforting when she had hers.

She hadn't had a nightmare in years, though. Probably because her memories of the time before Mom and Dad adopted her had faded. She shivered again, wondering why she'd started thinking about those fleeting flashes of a face or voices...

What could her old memories have to do with the current murders? Nothing.

Maybe she was just looking for something to think about besides her tenuous relationship with Troy. They spent so much time apart, and whenever she tried to talk about the future, he either ignored her like he had the past few weeks or he insisted they needed to wait until he saved more money.

Lakin was getting tired of waiting. While she had no intention of buying herself an engagement ring, especially with the Fiancée Killer on the loose, she had bought herself something else. And she wasn't a damn bit sorry. She wanted Troy to share her dreams, but if he wasn't ready, it didn't matter. She wasn't putting her dreams on hold anymore, not even for him.

The thought made her sick again, and she was glad she was drawing closer to her cabin. She'd had some sleepless nights lately as she lay awake, listening for any suspicious sounds, for someone trying to get into her place.

The killer was making her paranoid, and she hated it. Hated feeling like she did now, chilled all of a sudden. Maybe the cabins she'd passed weren't all empty. Maybe someone had chosen to skip their adventure tour or had returned early.

Or maybe...

Maybe it wasn't a guest. Maybe someone really

was following her and scrutinizing her every move. She shivered, trying to shake off the paranoia. But she glanced back over her shoulder nonetheless.

The wind wriggled some tree branches, but nothing else moved behind her.

*Definitely paranoid.*

Smiling at herself, she let the tension drain away and slowed her approach to her cabin. She wouldn't be living here much longer if she had her way, so she took a moment to study the little wood structure tucked into a stand of pine trees. She and Troy had had so many magical moments in this place that she would miss it.

Like she missed him…

So damn much that she ached for him. Why hadn't he come inside the office earlier today? Why had he just driven off again without even a wave in her direction?

She blinked against the sudden rush of tears, and as she refocused, she noticed that her door wasn't shut tightly. A crack showed between it and the jamb. While she hadn't always locked her door, ever since hearing about the serial killer, she made certain that she closed and locked it.

Unless…

Was it Troy? She didn't see his truck parked anywhere, but maybe he'd hidden it to surprise her. But she didn't feel the way she usually felt when he was near; she didn't feel any tingling awareness of him.

She felt only fear.

\* \* \*

Hired assassins. Dead bodies and a serial killer. As Hetty brought Troy up to speed on what had been happening in Shelby, he was horrified and worried.

That morning Mitch had alluded to a lot happening lately in Shelby, but the lawyer hadn't had time to go into detail. He'd left for court right after his meeting with Troy. Troy wished Mitch would have filled him in on all this; he wouldn't have decided to catch up with his sister before seeing the woman he loved. The woman he was so damn worried about now.

Lakin lived alone in her little cabin that was too far from the other ones at RTA, too far away for someone to hear her cry for help, for someone to rescue her if she needed it.

Scared for her safety, he jumped up from his chair at the table he and Hetty were sharing at Roasters. Even this late in the day, the café was pretty busy with people using laptops or reading books while sipping from their bright blue Roasters coffee mugs.

"I need to check on Lakin," he told Hetty. While he'd wanted to give himself some time to figure out how to tell Lakin what happened on the oil rig, he wished now that he'd rushed right in to see her, to hold her, to assure himself that she was all right. That was all he wanted to do now, make sure that she was safe. He started toward the door.

"Hey," Hetty called after him. "You should have been worried about Lakin before this. You should have been worried about losing her."

Losing her?

Because he'd never been good enough for her? He'd known that for years; that was why he hadn't proposed yet. He wanted to be able to buy her a big engagement ring as well as that business she wanted to run with him. He wanted to be able to make all of her dreams come true.

Was that what Hetty was talking about? That Lakin was going to realize he wasn't good enough for her? Or that he might lose her to someone like the serial killer going after women in Shelby?

Right now he just wanted to make sure Lakin was safe, so he didn't bother to ask his sister to clarify. Instead, ignoring the twinge in his back, he hurried out of the café and hopped in his truck. Speeding back to RTA, Troy silently cursed himself for leaving earlier without talking to her.

While he appreciated his sister apprising him of everything that had happened while he was gone, she'd wasted her breath warning him about losing Lakin. He'd been worried about losing her ever since their first date.

But then he'd only been worried about losing her to someone who had more to offer her than he did. Now he was worried about all the other horrific ways that he could lose her.

He hoped Dawn Ellis was found soon. Hopefully she wouldn't be another victim of the serial killer.

A serial killer in their safe community. Hired assassins who'd shot Hetty.

What the hell was happening in the place he'd always considered the safest? While crime and chaos ruled in other areas, Shelby had always been quiet and controlled with nothing more than petty thefts and drunken disorderly conduct around town.

But now...

Now he just wanted to see Lakin, to hold her, to make sure that she was safe. He was so impatient that the truck tires squealed as he turned into the parking lot of RTA. Jumping out of his truck, he limped across the porch of the RTA office, pushed open the door and stepped inside, calling out, "Lakin! Lakin!"

Parker poked his head out of his office and grinned at him. "Hey, Troy, I'm damn glad to see you're home!"

The Coltons had always been so friendly and accepting of Troy even when they had to know that Lakin, with her beauty and intelligence, could do better than him. But that was the kind of people that they were. Lakin had once shared that their family motto was *believe.*

The motto had originated because of some tragedy from their past. But it meant that whenever someone told them something, they would believe them until proven otherwise. So maybe they believed he would make Lakin happy...until he proved them otherwise.

"I'm damn glad to be home," Troy said. And he was happy now that he was back if only just because of everything that had been going on while he was gone. Not to mention that he should just be damn happy that he was alive at all. "Where's Lakin?"

While he usually would have talked with Parker about RTA business and life in general, he'd already spent way too much time away from his love.

"Ouch," Parker said with a hand to his chest. "Thanks for making it clear I'm not the Colton you were hoping to find in the office." Instead of being offended, Parker chuckled. "I totally get it. I'm not the Colton who would like to be in the office."

Neither was Lakin but her brother didn't know that yet. She wasn't ready yet to leave, though. Or maybe she was, but Troy wasn't ready yet to help her leave the family business to start their own. If only he'd been able to save more money, but with help-ing his younger brother with college and his mother with living expenses, he hadn't been able to save as much as they needed yet. And now...if he wasn't able to work on the rigs anymore...

He couldn't even let himself think about that yet, about how he would make the kind of money he needed if he couldn't go back to work. Hopefully Mitch would come up with a plan for him to at least hold the oil company responsible for disability pay while Troy fully recovered from the fall.

"I don't care where Lakin is," Troy said. "I just want to see her."

Parker chuckled again. "You have been gone a long time."

"And Hetty's brought me up to speed on what's

been happening around Shelby while I was gone," Troy said to further explain his urgency to see the woman he loved.

Parker's smile slid away, and his body tensed. "Yeah, it's not been good."

"Or safe. So I really want to check on her, make sure she's okay," Troy explained.

Parker smiled again, but then he shivered as if he was chilled. "She just left a little while ago. She wasn't feeling well. I offered to see her back to her cabin, but she insisted she would be fine."

While her big brother might have believed that, Troy wasn't so sure. Nobody was safe with a killer on the loose in Shelby.

Eli Colton stared down at the young woman's body, but instead of seeing her, he saw his sister's face and his aunt's and his cousin's. Then he blinked away the horrors of his imagination and his memory and focused.

Dawn Ellis was someone's sister, someone's cousin, someone's daughter, and now she was dead.

He'd hoped like hell that she would be found alive, but just forty-eight hours after she'd been reported missing, she was found here, on the outskirts of Shelby. The town where Eli's dad and uncle had moved their families because they'd believed it would keep all of them safe from harm.

But here, just off the road, she'd been found—her body staged just like the other victims, with all but her head and left hand buried. She wore a gaudy fake ring, and she had the telltale marks around her neck from the hands of whoever had strangled her. When the rest of her body was uncovered, Eli had no doubt she would be wearing a little black dress. Like she'd just been at her engagement party.

But Dawn Ellis hadn't been engaged.

Three other bodies had been found buried just like this, wearing similar gaudy rings and black dresses. Only one of them had been identified, leaving two other Jane Does whose families were undoubtedly still looking for them.

Hopefully they would find DNA matches soon, so those people would have some peace, some closure, if there was actually such a thing.

Was it only Eli's imagination that had him comparing Dawn to the women he loved? All the victims had long, dark brown hair like his sister Lakin and his cousin Kansas and were roughly the same age. A lot of women had dark hair and were in their age range, though, so it was probably just a coincidence. Maybe it was just his fears making him draw comparisons to the women he cared about.

Thinking of Lakin and Kansas, Eli stepped away from the crime scene that the techs were meticulously processing to make some calls. To make sure that everyone he loved was safe.

Kansas picked up immediately. "You found her?" she asked. She was in law enforcement, too, and clearly knew why he would randomly check up on her.

"Yes."

"Where?"

He gave her the location. "I'll talk to you when you get here," he said. He glanced at his partner Asher, wondering if he should warn him that his nemesis was going to be here soon. Kansas and Asher did not get along, often putting Eli in the middle of their squabbles. He loved them both too much to take sides, but he often tried to point out at they were all actually on the same side.

Enforcing the law. While he and Asher were lieutenants in the major crimes division of the Alaska Bureau of Investigations, Kansas was a state trooper and member of the search and rescue unit.

But he would warn Asher in a minute that Kansas was on her way. Right now he had another call to make.

But his call to Lakin went unanswered.

Lakin always answered her phone. Where was she? And was she okay?

# *Chapter 3*

Her cell ringing startled Lakin, but she wasn't the only one. A clang rang out from behind the partially open door to her cabin. She gasped. Somebody was definitely inside.

"Troy?" she called out tentatively.

It had to be Troy. Right? He'd been at the office earlier. When he drove off without talking to her, he could have been planning to surprise her at home.

And yet she hesitated before walking into her own cabin. It didn't feel like her home right now; it felt unfamiliar, strange…like her relationship with Troy had suddenly become.

He'd never gone so long with so little contact before. Something had to be wrong, and she knew that he wouldn't try to remedy that with a surprise. And if he'd wanted to surprise her, he wouldn't have sent the email last week letting her know that he was finally coming home.

But home probably just meant Shelby. Despite how much he stayed with her when he wasn't working, they didn't live together. Most of his things and his room were at his mother's house. Mrs. Amos undoubtedly missed her son as much as Lakin did. And she probably worried about him even more since she'd lost her husband on the same oil rigs that her son insisted on working on as well.

Lakin wasn't sure if he was just trying to help his family out or if he missed his father so much that he was trying to replace him. Either way, she loved him for loving all of them so much.

But as much as she loved him, she was beginning to lose hope for a future with him.

So she didn't believe he'd made the noise inside the cabin. Something…or someone…else was in there.

Once a raccoon had managed to break in through an open window. But a door? As clever and capable as they were with their little handlike paws, she doubted that was possible.

No, it had to be a human inside her place.

But who? Why would anyone break in? She had nothing worth stealing. The only things of value were her heart, which Troy already had, and her life.

She started backing away from the cabin, scared that whoever was inside was going to come out. She turned to run but instead collided with a long, hard body. She gasped as strong arms wrapped around her.

But these arms were familiar.

"Hey, what's wrong?" Troy asked, his voice a low rumble in his muscular chest.

She tingled with awareness of his closeness and with fear. "Someone's in my cabin," she whispered.

How was Troy here? She'd been so focused on her cabin that she hadn't heard his truck drive up.

"Run back to the office," Troy whispered gruffly. Maybe he didn't want to alert the intruder to their presence—but her ringing cell had already done that. He turned with her in his arms, positioning himself between her and the cabin, then released her. "Go," he urged her. "Get Parker and call the police."

The police—well, her brother Eli—had already called. But she'd been so stunned to find her door open that she hadn't known how to react.

As if Troy expected her to obey him, he turned back toward her front door.

"Where are you going?" she asked, her voice rising slightly with panic.

"I'm going to try to catch whoever the hell is in there." He started toward the door again.

"No, it's too dangerous. They could have a gun or some kind of weapon," she warned and reached out, trying to stop him.

But then another noise rang out, louder than their argument: the crack of the cabin's back door slamming.

Before Lakin could grasp his arm, Troy was off, running after a figure that was just a blur of dark clothes heading into the woods. But Troy wasn't really running. Not like he usually did. He was moving oddly, stiffly, like he was limping or hurt.

If he caught up with the intruder, he might get hurt even worse.

The shadow was tall and broad and moving faster than Troy. But if the person turned back, they could overpower Troy, especially if they were armed. If they were armed, they might do more than just overpower him.

"Troy!" she yelled, her heart racing with fear. "Troy! Come back!"

But it was too late. He disappeared into the woods. Would it be the last time she saw him?

Troy ignored the twinges of pain in his back as he pushed himself to run faster through the forest. Branches were rustling and snapping back toward him; he was close to whoever had come out of Lakin's cabin. But all he could see was a dark shadow through the trees.

A black coat maybe? Black hat? Hiking boots. He could tell by the deep treads pushing the pine needles into the dirt.

Just about everybody in Shelby wore hiking boots, though, and coats and hats, too, since the evenings were cold in September. It could have been anyone, and too many trees and branches blocked Troy from getting a better look at the person. He had to get closer. But as he ran harder, the uneven ground twisted his back, and he winced.

"Stop!" he yelled at the intruder like Lakin had yelled after him. But he didn't expect this person to listen to him any more than he had listened to her.

Troy had to find out who'd broken into her place

and why. Was this the person Hetty had told him about? The serial killer targeting women in Shelby? Even though he and Lakin had been in a relationship for ten years, she was alone so much. Was that why someone had broken into her place?

Was she the serial killer's next target?

Frustration gripped him, making his muscles tense even more, and he had to stop running for a moment. He had to catch his breath. His lungs burning, he leaned forward, hands on his thighs and drew in deep breaths of fresh air.

Fresh air with a hint of stale cigarette smoke. Usually the woods smelled of pine needles and fresh rain. The intruder had to be close.

Troy peered around, wondering where the person was hiding. Maybe they weren't hiding at all. Maybe they were waiting to ambush him once he got close.

He didn't want to get knocked out, or worse, and leave Lakin unprotected. Hopefully she had run back to the office to get Parker and had called the local police. Eli and Kansas could be anywhere in Alaska, but Shelby PD was close. And at the moment Troy was more of a liability than an asset. Instead of saving her from the intruder, he might need saving himself.

The man ducked under the pine boughs and hunkered down near the trunk. He shouldn't be discovered in the shadows. And if he was…

Maybe that would be a good thing. Getting rid of whoever was chasing him would be the smart thing to do. He couldn't afford for someone to disrupt the plan he had painstakingly put into place. He had put in too much effort and research for it to be put into jeopardy now.

Who the hell was this guy anyway?

He'd not been around the past few weeks, not like the other men, those *Coltons*. They were always around. The boys and their dad. He would deal with them in time, too.

But right now…

Now he had a more immediate problem. This young stranger had rushed headlong to her rescue, chasing after him through the woods. Except… there was no running now. No snapping of twigs and branches or rustling of leaves. Just what sounded like gasps for breath.

Whoever was trying to be her hero either wasn't in very good condition or wasn't used to the altitude.

It would be easy now to take him out. He would never become a problem.

# Chapter 4

Troy was hurt. Lakin knew it even before she found him gasping for breath in the middle of the forest. She'd recognized pain on his face as he took off after the intruder. His entire long body looked as if it had protested every step he took.

"What's wrong?" she asked when she found him. "What's happened?"

She would have thought that the intruder had turned the tables on Troy and attacked him, but there were no visible marks on his smooth chocolate skin, no swelling on his handsome face. He looked as perfect as always but for the pain in his beautiful green eyes. His mouth twisted into a grimace, and finally he released a long breath and straightened up.

"What are you doing here?" he asked. "You were supposed to go to Parker, to the office, to safety..." He glanced at the trees around them, as if expecting the intruder to be hiding nearby.

Maybe they were; Lakin could smell something other than the pines, something like stale cigarette smoke. She felt that strange sensation again, like she was being watched. She shivered and whispered, "We should go back to the cabin."

"You should," Troy said, and he put his hand against the small of her back, turning her away from him. "Go back to the cabin. Now."

"Not without you," she said. "You're hurt. What happened?" Why wouldn't he just admit that he'd been injured and tell her how? Not that they had time to talk here. They needed to get out of here, but Lakin wasn't leaving without Troy.

"I'm fine," he said. But his jaw was so clenched, she was surprised he managed to get out the lie. He clearly wasn't fine.

"Troy!" she exclaimed with exasperation.

Branches rustled around them; something was moving in the trees.

Troy pulled Lakin into his arms and wrapped them around her, as if using his body to shield her from whatever was coming.

But no person appeared.

Maybe when she shouted at him, she'd startled a bird or something. Or maybe it had been just a sudden gust of wind.

She could feel Troy's heart beating fast and hard, could feel the heat of his skin, the hardness of his muscled body. This was where she should have been, in his arms, the minute he got back into town.

But he hadn't come straight to her. And then someone had been inside her damn cabin. Doing what?

"I called Parker and Eli," she assured him and

whoever might be out there listening to them. She felt that strange sensation again, that creepy awareness of someone watching her. Who was it?

The intruder in her cabin proved that she wasn't just imagining things. Someone could really be following her around. If not for Troy showing up when he had, they might have gotten her.

She wound her arms around him now and held on. But as she tightened her grasp around his back, he flinched.

"You are hurt," she said. "Troy—"

"Lakin!" Parker's voice echoed around the woods. "Troy! Where are you?"

"Here, we're here!" she called back to her brother.

"The police are on their way," Parker said loudly, as if warning off whoever might be hiding in the woods with them.

Lakin was pretty sure that someone was out there, watching them, waiting… For what? For her to be alone?

Branches rustled again, but it was Parker who pushed them aside. "Thank God you two are all right," he said. "Who was it? Did you see them?"

Troy shook his head.

"I saw the front door of the cabin was open," Lakin explained, "so I didn't go inside. And when the intruder ran out the back, I just saw a shadow heading toward the woods."

"It was a good thing you noticed the door was

open," Parker said. He shuddered as if horrified over what could have happened to her.

"I'm sure it wasn't…" *The serial killer*, she thought. But she didn't say the words out loud. She didn't want to think of him or give him any more attention. Wasn't that why serial killers killed? They wanted the notoriety and attention? The press had already given him a name, had already reported too much about him.

But not everything.

They didn't know what had happened years ago within the Colton family. They didn't know how eerily close the crimes felt to one that had almost destroyed her family before she'd even become part of it.

Her family was strong and resilient. They had not allowed that tragedy to define them. But if someone brought that tragedy to the attention of the press, they might make her family relive it all over again.

"Let's head back to the office," Parker said. "Shelby PD's finest, Bobby Reynolds, is on his way, and Eli and Kansas are, too. We'll leave the policing to all of them."

"And leave the chasing after bad guys to them, too," Lakin said pointedly to Troy. "You shouldn't have gone after him. What if he'd had a weapon?"

He shrugged. "I just wanted to see who it was."

"Eli will figure that out," Parker said.

Lakin worried that everybody expected too much of her oldest brother but nobody more so than Eli himself. He had so much responsibility bearing down on him; she didn't want to add to his burden. But she did want to know who the hell had been in her place, just not badly enough to chase after them herself.

With her arm around Troy, she urged him from the woods. Parker fell behind them, as if making sure that nobody could sneak up on them. Proof that Parker wasn't any more willing to leave everything up to his older brother than Lakin was. He was trying to protect her, too, just as all her brothers had always done, Eli, Mitch and Parker.

Troy had always wanted to protect her, too. But she wondered now if the one she really needed the most protection from was him.

Going so long without seeing him or even communicating with him had hurt her. Badly. And it had hurt their relationship to the point where Billy Hoover and Eric Seller weren't the only ones questioning it.

Like those men, she was also wondering if there was a future for the two of them. Did Troy love her as much as he once had? Did he love her enough to start their future now instead of waiting? Because Lakin was tired of waiting.

The deaths of those young women, including the aunt she'd never met, proved to her that life could be cut much too short.

"What the hell happened to you?" Parker asked. It was the same question that Lakin had asked Troy in the woods.

The three of them had made it back to the RTA office, even locking themselves inside the building. But despite the sound of sirens growing louder, Troy didn't feel any safer than he had in the woods. Because now both Lakin and her brother were staring at him.

The muscles in his back were cramping up again, making him flinch despite his best effort to ignore the pain. He didn't want Lakin to find out about his fall off the oil rig like this. He wanted the time and the privacy to explain why he hadn't called her or his family.

"Did the guy get the jump on you out there?" Parker asked. "You said you didn't see him but…"

"I didn't see him, and he didn't attack me," Troy said. "I don't even know if it was a man or a woman."

"Troy was already limping before he ran after the intruder," Lakin said. "But he won't tell me what happened to him."

Drawing it out was just making her angrier, he could see that. She would also be angry that he hadn't told her when it happened, just like Hetty. His mom and other siblings would probably also be pissed at him.

"I fell off the oil rig several weeks ago," he said. And he'd missed all those weeks of pay. Hopefully Mitch could help him get reimbursed for those lost wages.

Lakin's dark eyes widened with shock. "You fell into the water? How? What happened?"

He shrugged and flinched again at the twinge of pain in his back. "I don't know. I thought my safety harness was secure, but the cable or something snapped when I was up on one of the towers, and I fell and hit the water." So damn hard.

Parker gasped. "You could have died."

Troy knew that all too well; it was how his father had died. "I didn't. I'm fine," he said, trying to reassure Lakin. Her dark eyes were still so wide, and her face was pale.

"You're not fine," she said, sounding like she was gritting her teeth. "You're limping, and you're obviously in pain right now."

Running on uneven ground hadn't been good for his back. But hopefully the physical therapy he'd signed up for in town would make it easier for him to use his muscles again.

"I'm better," he said. "For a while..." He trailed off and not just because the sirens were even louder now as the police pulled into the parking lot.

He didn't want to say any more about his accident, at least not until he and Lakin were alone. Knowing how protective her family was of her, he wondered if he would get the chance anytime soon. But keeping her safe was more important than anything else, even their relationship.

And let alone keep her safe, right now, he didn't know if he could help her achieve all those dreams she had, not without knowing how well he might heal.

But why was she in danger? Who the hell had

broken into her cabin? Was the serial killer targeting Lakin now?

The thought horrified him more than anything else. He couldn't imagine anyone wanting to hurt Lakin. And he didn't want to imagine anyone succeeding.

Eli looked at his sister and saw Dawn Ellis's lifeless face instead. The color drained from her skin, the blue around her painted red lips and that garish ring on the finger of her exposed hand.

Then he blinked and saw Lakin again. She was moving carefully through the cabin that Eli and his team had already searched with the help of the local police department. Officer Reynolds wasn't really thrilled that they'd taken over, but he hadn't argued. He knew how close the Coltons stuck together; he just didn't know why. He didn't know what they'd already been through and how many loved ones they'd already lost, albeit nearly three decades ago.

"Is anything missing?" Eli asked Lakin.

She stopped in the kitchenette; the doors of the few hickory wood cupboards stood open. The refrigerator door had been open, too, but someone had closed it after processing the handle for prints and DNA. Probably Scott Montgomery. The tech was detail-oriented like that and wouldn't have wanted any of her food to spoil.

"When I saw my front door was open and heard someone inside, I thought of the raccoon who got through the window last year," Lakin said with a small smile.

"It wasn't a raccoon who jimmied open the door," Eli said. Though, since she hadn't dead-bolted it, the lock wouldn't have been hard to open.

"But this seems like someone scavenging, doesn't it?" she said, pointing at the food that had been dropped on the floor as well as on the small table. "Maybe they were looking for something to eat, not for me."

Eli hoped like hell that was the case. After all, none of the other crime scenes had been left a mess like this. Not that the women had been murdered where their bodies were found. He had yet to find the actual crime scenes. He shrugged. "It doesn't make sense."

Kansas nodded in agreement.

Officer Reynolds sighed and pushed a hand through his short brown hair. "There have been a couple other break-ins like this in the area," he said. "People who are out of work and desperate to make ends meet. Like I said, I don't think this is a case for major crimes or search and rescue." His dark eyes narrowed as he shot a glance at both Eli and Kansas.

"There are food banks," Eli said. He didn't believe there was any excuse to commit a crime. And if someone was desperate for food, why break into a small cabin that might have only been used for vacationers? It could have been empty or poorly stocked.

Unless they'd been watching it for a while, watching Lakin.

"Well, some people are too proud to admit they need help," Kansas said.

"Some people are too proud for their own damn good," Lakin muttered just loudly enough for Eli to hear and wonder. She was staring through the window to where Troy stood outside next to Parker.

He'd noticed the tension between them from the minute he walked into the office over an hour ago. Usually when Troy was around, the two of them couldn't stop grinning and laughing; it was like love bubbled out of them.

"Are you mad because he tried to chase down the intruder?" he asked.

She hesitated a moment, then nodded.

Was that really the reason for the tension between them? Eli could understand her being upset that Troy had put himself in danger like that. Eli would have been upset, too, but he understood why Troy had gone after the guy. Troy loved Lakin as much as her family did. Maybe more.

Troy really looked sick, his face twisted with a grimace. Probably because he hadn't caught the guy. Eli understood that feeling all too well, too. He had to catch this damn serial killer before he took anyone else's life, anyone else's loved one.

Fortunately, Eli didn't think that was who'd broken into Lakin's place. "What do you think, Kansas?" he asked his cousin. "Is Officer Reynolds right? This intruder is just somebody down on their luck looking for food or cash?"

His cousin nodded.

But Eli caught a look passing over Lakin's face, like she had something else to say.

"What is it?" he asked her. "Is something else bothering you?"

She shook her head. "No, I think I'm just letting all the press about that killer get to me."

"Sometimes it's good to be scared," Kansas said. "It makes you more aware and cautious. You noticed that door before you got too close to the cabin. That's good."

It was good to be aware and cautious, but that didn't mean it would keep a person safe. Eli had a horrible feeling that this killer might just consider awareness a challenge. But hopefully Officer Reynolds and Kansas were right and that was not who had broken into Lakin's place. Finding another body had probably just put Eli too on edge to accept a simple explanation for the break-in.

Hopefully nobody was after Lakin at all. And the only thing she needed to be concerned about was whatever was going on between her and Troy.

## *Chapter 5*

Lakin knew she should have told Eli about the strange feeling she'd been having that someone was watching her. But after seeing her place and realizing that all the intruder had taken was some food, she'd gone back to feeling paranoid instead of genuinely worried about being stalked. She had no proof that anyone was really watching her, just a sensation she sometimes got. The only proof she had of any crime was of someone being so desperate for food that they'd broken in to steal some.

Eli and Kansas had much more dangerous criminals to find than her hungry intruder. So once the techs finished processing her cabin for prints on the doorknob and the kitchen cabinets, she hugged them both and sent them back to their more important cases. She earned a smile of approval from Officer Reynolds, who seemed so serious that he probably rarely smiled.

"I'll be fine," she assured her brother and her cousin. "And I'll make sure that I use the dead bolt now on all the doors even when I'm not home." Nobody would have gotten inside if she had.

Eli hugged her again and whispered, "Please, be careful, little sis."

She hugged him back and promised, "I will."

She wasn't sure if his concern was only regarding the serial killer or if he'd noticed the tension between her and Troy as well. Eli never missed a thing, though, so he was probably cautioning her about both.

When he and Kansas followed Officer Reynolds out of Lakin's cabin, she began to close the door, but a hand caught the edge of it.

Troy stepped inside with her. Then he closed and dead bolted the door behind himself.

The tension was there, but it wasn't just frustration she felt now. She also felt the usual awareness, the attraction. Despite all the years they'd been together, she'd never gotten used to the rush of desire she felt for him. Maybe if their relationship hadn't been long distance so many of those years, she would have gotten used to it. But he'd never given her the chance.

"Do Eli and Kansas think they'll be able to find the intruder?" Troy asked.

She shrugged. "I think he's the least of their concerns right now."

"But he broke in here—"

"Apparently because he or she was hungry," she said, gesturing toward the kitchenette. She still had to clean up the food on the floor, the table and in the sink, as well as the residue from the fingerprinting.

"They still broke into *your* home," he said, his voice gruff with emotion, "and if you had been home—"

"They probably would have gone on to the next cabin," she interjected.

"Parker checked the other ones," Troy said. "He couldn't find any sign that anyone had tried getting into them. Just yours."

That knowledge chilled her a bit. Why just hers? Maybe because hers was the farthest away from the others, so the chance of getting caught was slimmer. She hoped that was the only reason, but she wasn't going to obsess over that, not right now. She was obsessing over something else, over some*one* else.

She shrugged off his concerns about the break-in. "I don't want to talk about that right now. I want to know how badly you were hurt when you fell off the oil rig." Several weeks ago. Several weeks ago he'd been hurt, but he hadn't let her know. Why? Because he hadn't been able to? But why didn't someone from the oil company contact his family?

Troy sighed and rubbed his hand over the head of black hair he kept super short. "Lakin…"

"Tell me," she insisted. "How bad did you get hurt when you fell off the rig?"

He touched his back almost unconsciously, like he didn't realize he was doing it. "I… I was paralyzed."

"You were *paralyzed*?" she repeated, her voice

cracking. Pain pressed on her chest, making her heart ache for what he must have gone through. "Why didn't you call me, Troy? I would have rushed to the hospital—"

"That's why," he said. "I didn't want to put you or my family through the fear and uncertainty—"

"That you were feeling," she interjected. She couldn't imagine how scared he'd been. That he hadn't reached out to his family didn't make her feel any better. She loved his mother and siblings almost as much as she loved him, almost as much as she loved her own family. "You shouldn't have had to go through that all by yourself."

"I wanted to," he said. "*I* had to know what I was facing before I told anyone what happened."

"Why?" she asked, her heart pounding hard with fear, over what he'd gone through and over what it meant to their relationship that he'd chosen to be alone. "You have to know that it wouldn't have mattered to me or to your family. We would have wanted to be there for you no matter the outcome from your fall."

He groaned and rubbed his hand over his head again. "That was why, Lakin. I didn't want you or my family to make sacrifices for me—"

"Like you make?" she interjected. "You sacrificed your college education to go right to work on the oil rigs so you could help your mom and siblings." She'd understood that then. But what she had assumed would be just a few years had become seven, nearly eight years of long distance. "And you choose to keep working there instead of starting a business with me."

"Because I don't have enough money saved yet for us to give up our day jobs and start up a business," he said. "We have to be sure we have enough reserves to give us time to get the business up and running."

While Troy hadn't physically gone away for college like she had, Lakin knew that he took online courses in business. He probably knew more than she did even though she had the degree. And he wasn't going to agree with what she'd done any more than she agreed with what he'd done.

But right now, even though it made her feel like a hypocrite, she couldn't confess to what she'd done. She was too upset over his injury. That concerned her more than anything else. She hated that he'd been hurt even more than she hated that he'd chosen to go through his medical ordeal alone.

"So what are you facing?" she asked him. "You're obviously still in pain, still limping…"

He nodded. "I'm still healing. The swelling went down, and the paralysis went away, so I can start physical therapy now. But I still have some numbness and tingling, and I have to be careful until I'm completely healed or…"

"It could come back," she said, alarm shooting through her. "The paralysis could return?" She couldn't imagine Troy, who'd always been so strong and fit, feeling that helpless. He must have been terrified; he probably still was. She didn't dare show him how scared she was for him.

He shrugged, then grimaced slightly, as if the movement had tweaked those healing muscles again. "I don't know," he said. "I'm not even sure if the doctors know for sure, but they warned me that I have to be careful."

"Chasing after intruders wasn't being careful," she pointed out. Anger joined her fear. "You shouldn't have done that." And not just because of his back. He could have wound up in the hospital again or worse if the intruder had been dangerous.

She wasn't only angry that he'd put his life in danger again. She was angry that he'd shut her out. "And you shouldn't have kept what happened to you from me and your family," she said.

She was so damn hurt that he had. While she hadn't had the chance to tell him what she'd done, the two things were not the same. He'd been hurt and hadn't reached out to her for comfort or emotional support.

He reached out for her now, but she stepped back and shook her head. If he touched her, the same thing would happen that always happened. She would forget all about how she felt when he was gone and focus only on how wonderful it was that he was home, that he was with her again. While they always made the most of their time together, it was never long enough. He always went back to the oil rigs.

The thought of him going back again to where

he'd been hurt…and knowing that he could be hurt again or, worse, wind up dead like his dad, filled her with more terror than finding out someone had broken into her cabin.

"Lakin…" His voice was gruff with emotion, and his beautiful green eyes glistened with it. But was it regret? Did he feel bad for not contacting her?

"Why, Troy?" she asked. "Why did you shut me out?"

"Because I love you," he said.

She shook her head again. "No. You would have wanted me there with you then." He had kept her in the dark and at a distance for far too long. She'd wondered before how long they could continue that way, but now she realized it might already be too late to salvage their relationship.

Troy's arms ached to hold Lakin, but she kept stepping back from him, as if he was one of the bullies who used to pick on her on the playground. But he'd been the one who'd protected her from them, just like he'd wanted to protect her from what had happened to him.

He knew that she would have been upset and scared for him; he could see that she was now, just from hearing about his fall. He'd wanted to save her and his family from the uncertainty and fear of his paralysis. But apparently he'd only put it off; he hadn't saved her from it.

And he really hadn't saved her from the intruder

he'd chased through the woods. The person probably would have run off anyway if they had just been desperate for food, like Eli and Kansas seemed to think. Although if they had really wanted only food from her, they would have just had to ask. Lakin was so sweet and selfless that she would give someone her last morsel of food even if she was hungry, too.

"I do love you," he said, his heart aching. He reached out again to touch her cheek, to slide his fingertips across her soft skin. "I love you so much."

Tears filled her dark eyes, and she shook her head again. One of the tears slipped down her cheek, and he wiped it away with his fingertips. He hated that she doubted his feelings. He hated even more that he'd hurt her.

"I am so sorry," he said. "I just didn't want to put you and my mom through that uncertainty. I wanted to know what I was facing before I told anyone what happened." It had made sense at the time. But now...

"What are we facing, Troy?" she asked. "What kind of relationship do we have if we're not there for each other in the bad times as well as the good times?"

He sucked in a breath, alarmed at the question. Had she had doubts before about their relationship, or were her doubts new...and because of what he'd done?

"I'm sorry I didn't call you," he said.

"If you had it all to do over again, would you?" she asked. "Would you call me if you get hurt again?"

"Lakin…" He couldn't lie to her.

She stepped back again so that his hand dropped back to his side. "You should leave."

"But…" She had never turned him away before. In fact she was the one who usually pulled him inside this cabin with her, who led him toward the bed. But today she hadn't even kissed him yet.

Of course there'd been the intruder, and now… He wasn't sure what was going on now. His body was aching, but it wasn't just because of the fall. He wanted her, needed her, and she was turning him away for the first time in their lives.

Like he'd turned her away? Was she getting back at him for not calling her?

No. Lakin wasn't petty. She was kind and forgiving and loving.

And maybe he'd taken all of that for granted for much too long.

"You shouldn't be alone tonight," he said. "What if the intruder comes back?"

She shook her head. "They won't. They got food. Lunch meat and chips and cookies. It was probably a teenager. Maybe a runaway." Her brow furrowed, and her dark eyes glittered again with more tears, sympathy for the person who'd robbed her.

That was how sweet Lakin was.

And sometimes naive.

"Teenagers can still be dangerous," he pointed out.

That shadow he'd chased through the woods had been big and broad. Even if the intruder was a teenager, he was bigger and more muscular than Lakin, probably than Troy was right now. Hopefully the physical therapy he was starting in Shelby would get him back in shape soon, as well as get rid of the limp and the pain. It was frustrating enough that he couldn't work right now, but it was even more frustrating that he couldn't really protect the woman he loved.

"I'm going to dead bolt the doors like I promised Eli I would," she said. "I'll be fine."

"I won't," he said. "Not with you mad at me. I won't leave you here alone. I'll be outside in my truck." He turned and started for the door. Standing in one place had stiffened his back even more, making his limp more pronounced. He grimaced at the twinge of pain.

"Don't go," she said.

He released a breath of relief. Another thing he loved about Lakin was that she could never stay angry for long. She was always quick to forgive. Maybe he'd been counting on that when he hadn't called her.

But then she said begrudgingly, "You can sleep on the couch."

Before he could even turn around, he heard the door to the bedroom close and then lock.

He'd shut her out when he hadn't called her after his fall, but he'd done so out of consideration. He hadn't wanted to worry her until he knew what he was facing. But she was shutting him out now, and he wasn't sure why.

Was she just too angry to forgive him yet? Or was she completely over him?

Another body was found.

Will stared down at the text on his phone, but the sudden rush of tears blinded him for a moment as he thought of Caroline. Of how he and Eli had found his beautiful sister sitting with her killer, both deceased, on the couch in the home where Eli had grown up, where he'd once felt so safe. It hadn't been safe for any of his family that day. His parents had been murdered in their bed. And his dear sweet baby sister had been strangled to death at seventeen.

But it wasn't her body that had been found today. It had to be the woman who'd been reported missing: Dawn Ellis.

Poor Dawn and her family. Her poor family.

Will knew all too well the devastating heartbreak they would be suffering. He and his brother had suffered like that. On that one horrific day, they'd lost so much: their parents and their beautiful younger sister. All taken from them much too soon and much too cruelly.

"What is it?" asked Sasha, his beautiful wife.

He jumped a bit, startled by her sudden appearance. She'd been out in her studio, the one he'd built behind their house for her pottery. She was so damn talented. And beautiful. Her once light brown hair was silvery gray now, making her blue eyes even brighter in her delicately featured face.

"Eli sent a text," Will said.

"It upset you," she said.

"I think they found that missing woman," he said.

Eli was pretty careful to not give him too many details, but the ABI lieutenant always gave Will a heads-up so he wouldn't be surprised, like they'd both been surprised on that horrible, tragic day.

Sasha released a shaky sigh. "She's dead."

Will nodded. "I think it's her." Unless there was another victim. Two of the bodies that had already been discovered were yet to be identified. Somewhere, their families were probably hoping they would be found alive. But a killer had made certain that wasn't possible.

"Eli will catch him," Sasha said, and she slipped her arms around Will's waist.

He wound his arms around her, too. He wasn't sure if he was offering her comfort or taking it. Or both. "I hope soon," he whispered. He didn't want anyone else to suffer the way his family had, the way the families of these recent victims had to be suffering.

"I need you to be careful," he said as he pressed a kiss to the top of her head.

She tipped her head up and smiled reassuringly at him. "I do not fit that profile. I'm not a young woman with brown hair." Her smile slipped away, probably with the realization he'd come to a while ago.

Lakin and Kansas were young dark-haired women. While his niece was armed and prepared to defend herself, Lakin was more vulnerable, if just because of her open, trusting heart. And she was alone so much; Troy was gone for work more than he was in Shelby. Will loved Troy like one of his children, but he wished the man would settle down with Lakin, especially given the current circumstances.

"We should have Lakin move back home for a while," he suggested. Then he could keep an eye on both her and his beautiful wife.

Sasha nodded and released a shaky breath that was warm against his throat. "Yes, that would be good."

If Lakin agreed…

But he had a feeling that if Lakin moved, it wasn't going to be back home. It would be into the new enterprise she was starting. He felt a rush of excitement for her over that and was glad she'd reached out to him for help, though it was their little secret for now.

He didn't know if that was because she wasn't ready yet to tell Parker that she was leaving the business or because she wasn't ready yet to tell Troy what she'd done.

But at this moment the most important thing was to keep her safe.

# *Chapter 6*

Guilt gripped Lakin for making Troy sleep on the couch. His back was injured, and he was too long for the sofa. While it was better than if he'd tried to sleep in his truck like he'd threatened, she should have given him her bed. But she would have been tempted to share it with him if she hadn't closed and locked the door between them.

There was nothing between them now as she stood over the couch and stared down at him. His handsome face was relaxed, no grimace on it as he was curled up on his side. He looked fine. Too fine for her to resist, so she hurried past him and out the door, closing it softly behind herself so she wouldn't wake him up.

So she didn't lean down and brush her mouth across his firm lips. She didn't run her hands over his muscular chest. She didn't straddle him on the sofa and make love to him like she wanted. She wanted him so much, but she felt as if the only reason he'd stayed was to protect her.

She didn't need him to take care of her; she needed

him to let her take care of him for once. But even
when he'd been hurt, he hadn't reached out for her
help. And that hurt her so much.

She wanted to be there for him like he tried to
be for her. But he hadn't tried that hard lately. He'd
been gone so much.

While he was sleeping peacefully, she hadn't been
able to rest at all the night before. The break-in had
rattled her, and even though she was comforted that
she wasn't alone in the cabin, she hadn't been able to
sleep. Troy was so close, yet not close enough. She'd
wanted him beside her, his arms wrapped around her,
her head against his chest.

Maybe she should have unlocked her door and
asked him to join her in bed. But they wouldn't have
slept then, either. And all that passion would have
clouded her judgment even more.

Because she hadn't slept, she headed straight to
Roasters, in desperate need of caffeine.

That wasn't likely to assuage her guilt, though.
She didn't feel guilty just over making Troy sleep
on the couch; she felt guilty over being mad at him
for keeping things from her when she was doing the
same. She was a hypocrite because she hadn't told
him yet what she'd done about the auction of the
Shelby Hotel.

She would talk to him. After her coffee…

It was earlier than she usually stopped at the café,
so hopefully she wouldn't run into Billy Hoover or
Eric Seller. The last thing she needed was either of

them asking about her future with Troy again when she was so uncertain of it herself. She would probably burst into tears if they questioned her about her relationship today.

She was tired of waiting for Troy to be present in their relationship. She wanted to start their lives instead of just planning for a future that seemed to never arrive. And she wanted him to want that, too.

The guilt she'd felt earlier dissipated some. She had every right to be angry with him. She was also too hurt and proud to welcome him back with open arms like she did every time he came home after a long time working away.

Although he hadn't been just working this time; he'd been hurt.

She hated thinking of him lying alone in a hospital bed waiting for paralysis to go away, worrying that it wouldn't. He must have been terrified.

But he was the one who'd chosen to go through all that on his own. If he'd let her or his family know, they would have been there to support him. To love him…

Did he no longer want her love or support?

She needed to ask him these questions instead of asking them of herself. But first she needed her coffee.

She easily found a spot to park her SUV. Roasters wasn't that busy yet. There were only a few other patrons sitting at the tables, and one couple was in line in front of her when she walked into the café with two bright blue Roasters mugs. Troy had one that he left at her place.

She almost wished the line was longer. Then she would have more time to think about how to talk to Troy. She needed to get through to him that if he loved her, he should let her be there for him. And then she had to tell him what she'd done when she hadn't been able to reach him.

She released a small sigh that drew Fay, the barista's attention. "Coffee's coming, Lakin. I just brewed a fresh pot when I saw your SUV pull up outside."

She passed both mugs over the counter. "I need two today, please," she said just as a yawn slipped out.

The younger woman nodded. "I understand why. I didn't sleep at all last night, either, not after hearing that terrible news about poor Dawn Ellis. I was really hoping she would be found alive."

Lakin gasped. "They found her?" Why hadn't Eli told her? Probably because they had to verify her identity and notify her family. Her poor family. "Are they sure it's her?"

The woman nodded. "Yeah, late yesterday just on the outskirts of town. They tried to keep the story from coming out, but someone must have leaked it."

Neither Eli nor Kansas had mentioned it yesterday, but then they'd been more concerned about Lakin and her intruder. And maybe they hadn't wanted to scare her any more than she already was. No wonder Kansas had kept advising her to be cautious.

"That's so sad," Lakin murmured, and she felt guilty again. She should have been happy that Troy was alive, that he hadn't been hurt worse. Instead she'd gotten hung up on how he hadn't called her when he'd been hurt. At least she and his family could see him again, could be with him. Unlike Dawn's family.

The barista sighed, and her eyes misted a bit. "We definitely need to be careful out there."

Lakin nodded. "Definitely." She was especially glad that Troy had spent the night. Even though she hadn't slept any better with him there than she probably would have without him, at least she'd been safe. "And please, make that second coffee a regular with a shot of espresso."

"You must be really tired this morning," the barista said with a smile. And then the young woman must have remembered—that was Troy's drink. "Oh…" Fay glanced around the restaurant "…that hot boyfriend of yours is back in town?"

Lakin nodded and tried not to be disappointed that after ten years, he was still only her boyfriend. Not her husband or even her fiancé. Apparently, she didn't need Billy Hoover or Eric Seller to ask about the future of her relationship; she was asking herself.

"I'll hurry it up so you can get right back to him," the barista promised.

A few minutes later, Lakin was trying to juggle both mugs and open the door when someone opened it for her. "Thanks," she said as she stepped out.

But instead of walking into Roasters, the man followed her to her truck parked at the curb just outside the café.

Her skin chilling with uneasiness, she looked up at him. He was tall with a rangy build, iron-gray hair and a lot of lines in his face. One of them was actually a scar, and it ran jagged down the left side of his face. Despite the wrinkles, he was probably just in his sixties, maybe even late fifties. While his hair was gray, his brows were black, like his eyes, and bushy.

Her uneasiness increased. She glanced into the café, hoping that the barista saw what was happening even though Lakin herself wasn't sure what this was.

"I can take it from here," she assured him. She set the coffee mugs on the roof of her SUV so that she could find her key fob in her purse. She wasn't sure if she would need it to unlock her doors or to sound the alarm button on it. There was something menacing about the man. Or maybe that was just her paranoia.

"Lakin," he said. "I've been looking for you for a long time, girl."

She tensed with even more fear. How did he know her name? How did he know her at all? "I… I don't know who you are," she said. And some instinct told her she really didn't want to know him.

He pressed his hand against his heart. "That hurts. But I guess I shouldn't be surprised. It's been a long time since I saw you, girl."

She shook her head. "I don't remember you."

"You were just a little girl," he said. "My little girl. I'm your father."

Instinctively she shook her head. Her father was handsome with kindness and gentleness that radiated from him. She glanced around, wishing he was running around town like usual. But he'd probably already been out for his morning run and was back home again with her beautiful mother.

She shook her head again, denying his claim. "No…"

He narrowed those beady dark eyes of his and leaned closer. "I am your biological father," he said. "You must know that you're adopted. You must remember me and your mother. You weren't a baby when you went missing."

"I didn't go *missing*," she said. "I was *abandoned*." And nobody had come looking for her. That was why the Coltons had been able to adopt her after they'd taken over fostering her. Nobody else had claimed her. "And I was only three years old."

"So you don't remember me at all?" he asked, suspicion in his dark eyes. "But I remember you, my sweet little girl." He smiled at her, but it didn't seem to quite reach his eyes.

Maybe he wasn't happy because she'd made it clear she didn't believe him. Should she? That was what Will and Sasha Colton had taught her; to give everyone the benefit of the doubt. To believe what they said until they were proven wrong. Because nobody had believed young Caroline Colton that she had a stalker…until it was too late.

Was this man a stalker? Was he the one who'd been watching Lakin?

He didn't look like he could be her father any more than the Coltons could be biologically related to her. From her darker complexion and hair and features, she was clearly part Inuit. This man wasn't. The only thing they had in common was the fact they both had dark eyes.

He reached into the pocket of his flannel shirt. "I got this," he said. "I've carried it with me for years, looking for you. And then to find you here…" He pulled out a photograph and held it out to her.

Her fingers shook as she reached for it. The colors had faded with age, leaving the photo in sepia tones, but the woman in it looked like Lakin. Her dark hair was long and straight and parted in the middle, high-lighting the same nose and mouth and cheekbones that Lakin had. That woman held a toddler who had dark hair and chubby cheeks, and she wore a lit-tle dress. The color was faded, but Lakin knew the dress was pink and came with ruffled underpants. The dress was tucked into a box somewhere in her cabin, the one thing she had left from that time be-fore the Coltons adopted her.

But it wasn't just the woman and the child in the photograph. A man stood next to them, almost tower-ing over them, casting them even more in shadow. He was tall and lean, and even in that photograph, he had a scar on one cheek. In the picture his hair matched the dark color of his bushy black brows. He looked younger but no happier. But then maybe he just didn't smile in photographs. Her brothers had gone through a phase where they had refused to smile, thinking they looked cooler with a scowl.

"That's me, your mama and you," he said, pointing a tobacco-stained fingertip at them. "Don't you remember us, Lakin? Your parents? Your real family?"

She shook her head again, not just because she didn't remember but because he was not her real family. The Coltons were. "No, I don't remember you."

"Well, that's a damn shame," he murmured. "Damn shame…"

She didn't remember him, and she didn't want to believe him although the family motto compelled her to. Her heart was beating fast and hard with fear. She didn't know if she was scared of him or scared of what he might tell her.

She had the urge to escape. To get away from him as fast as she could.

"I… I have to go," she said. "I'm going to be late for work."

"You don't want to talk to your daddy?" he asked with a slight smile as if he was more amused than offended. "You don't want to get to know me better?"

"I don't know you," she said. And despite her family motto, she was struggling to believe him. But that picture… She couldn't stop staring at it.

"Keep the photograph," he said. "I wrote my cell

number on the back. And when you're not so busy, you give me a call, and we can catch up on each other's lives since I lost you, little girl."

He made it sound like he'd just misplaced her somewhere, not like he'd abandoned her.

Unless…

Unless what she'd always believed was true was not what had really happened. What had really happened? Part of her had always wanted to know. So why not ask him? Why not talk to him?

She tore her gaze from the photo to look up, but he was gone. She glanced around, but she didn't see him anywhere. He'd left her again. Was that how he'd done it twenty-two years ago?

And what about her mother? Lakin glanced back at the picture. Where was she?

She flipped the photograph over and saw a phone number scrawled on the back of it along with a name: Jasper Whitlaw. Was that her father's name?

Was that her last name before it became Colton? Her first name had always been Lakin. She'd been talking at three, and she'd been able to tell people that. "Me…" And she would press her thumb in her chest. "…Lakin."

The Coltons often retold that story. But they'd never known her last name. Maybe she'd been too young to remember that.

"Whitlaw," she whispered it aloud, but it didn't sound familiar.

But the woman in the picture, she was definitely

familiar. It was like looking in a mirror. Her mother. Where was she? What was her name?

Lakin could call Jasper Whitlaw and ask him. But she wasn't sure she was ready yet for his answers. Or even to see him again. And at the moment, feeling as raw as she was, she wasn't sure she was ready to see Troy again, either.

Troy jolted awake with such a start that a grunt of pain slipped through his lips. He closed his eyes and tensed, waiting to see if he'd awakened Lakin. But there was no other sound in the cabin.

Maybe she was still ignoring him. He opened his eyes and peered around. The bedroom door wasn't locked anymore; it was wide open, so he could see that the bed was made. From the stillness of the cabin, he could tell that it was empty but for him.

She was gone.

He slowly sat upright and blinked to clear the sleep from his vision. The cabin was empty but bathed in sunshine. It wasn't as if she'd sneaked off in the middle of the night. Or worse yet, that someone had sneaked in and taken her.

She'd probably just left for work.

Usually when he came home from a long while away, she would take some personal days to spend time with him. The bed never got made because they rarely left it. Last night she hadn't even wanted him to touch her to comfort her, let alone kiss and make love with her.

He hadn't realized she would be so angry with him for not calling her when he was hurt. But if the situation was reversed…

He grimaced over a twinge of pain, but it was in his heart, not his back. If the situation was reversed, he would have been hurt, too, that she hadn't needed him and turned to him.

"Dammit," he murmured with sudden understanding of how badly he'd screwed up.

She was probably at the office by now, or maybe still at Roasters getting her morning coffee.

He slid his feet into his boots and stood to head to the door, but before he got there, the knob rattled.

The door opened, and Lakin stumbled across the threshold as if someone had pushed her.

"What's wrong?" he asked because she was clearly shaken. He glanced behind her to see if someone had chased her back to the cabin.

She shook her head.

"Where were you?" he asked.

She blinked at him as if she hadn't realized he was there, or maybe she didn't realize where she was. "I… I was at…at Roasters…"

He glanced at her hands. She wasn't holding the bright blue coffee mugs. Instead she clutched what looked like an old photograph in one hand.

"You don't have coffee, Lakin," he pointed out, keeping his voice soft and calm since she seemed so rattled.

Her dark eyes went wide. "I must have left the mugs on the roof of the SUV…"

"Is that why you look so stunned? You haven't had your caffeine fix yet?" he asked, trying to tease her a bit. Maybe she was still just really mad at him— and he understood now why.

She continued to stare at him with that blank expression, like she was in shock. She must have been to drive off with the mugs on the roof of her vehicle.

He was getting scared. "Lakin, what's wrong? What happened that you look so…" *Devastated.* He stepped close and put his hands on her shoulders.

This time she didn't jump back and shake off his touch like she had last night. It was as if she didn't even feel or see him. Her blank stare was unnerving.

"Lakin, I know you're still mad at me, but you have to talk to me," he persisted. "Or I'm going to call your parents or Eli—"

"No! Don't call my parents," she said, her voice cracking. Tears rushed to her eyes.

"Then talk to me," he said, his heart aching over the look on her beautiful face. He hated to see her cry. "Tell me why you're so shaken up right now. What happened? Did somebody bother you? Scare you?"

God, a serial killer was on the loose in Shelby. That scared the hell out of Troy. How had he fallen asleep last night? He hadn't done a very damn good job of protecting her when she'd managed to slip right past him this morning. He hadn't even realized she'd left. What if someone else had slipped past him and hurt her? He would never forgive himself if something happened to her whether he was here or not.

"Did you see the intruder again?" he asked when she still didn't answer. Maybe the person had tried getting into her vehicle and that was why she'd driven off like she had.

Her forehead furrowed as if she was trying to remember. "I… I don't think it was him…" she murmured.

"Him?" So she had seen someone. "Who are you talking about?"

She held out the photograph she'd been clutching. "Him…"

At first glance, Troy thought the woman in the picture was Lakin. They had the same hair, the same facial features that suggested Inuit heritage, but the snapshot was old, the colors faded. He turned it over to see if there was a date on it. Instead he saw a name and what must be a phone number scrawled across the back of it. "Jasper Whitlaw. Who is he?"

"He says he's my father," she whispered, as if she didn't want anyone to overhear what she said.

Troy thought immediately of her father, of Will Colton, with his tall, lean build and dark brown hair and bright blue eyes. He was probably pushing sixty, but he looked like he was in his forties.

Troy flipped the photograph back over and studied the man standing next to the woman who looked like Lakin. That man was lean, too, but in a way that was more hungry than fit. The scar on his cheek and the coldness in his dark eyes were nothing like the warmth in Will Colton's face, especially when Will was with his family. He loved them all so much, but Troy suspected he loved Lakin even a little more, maybe because he knew she needed more love.

Maybe Troy wasn't giving her enough love or time or attention. Hell, there was no maybe about it; he'd been neglecting the woman he loved. But that was because he was trying so hard to save for their future, so that he could buy her the ring she deserved to have, so he could help her finance the business she wanted to start.

After focusing on the woman in the photo and then the man, he turned his attention to the child. With her dark hair and dark eyes and little chubby cheeks, she was adorable. She could have been Lakin twenty some years ago.

"I've pretty much forgotten you were adopted," he admitted. She was so close to her family and so much a part of them that it didn't matter if they shared no DNA; they shared love.

But back in school other kids remembered the story of the little girl in the grocery store, and they hadn't let her forget about it…until Troy and her brothers made certain they stopped taunting her. Billy Hoover had taken a little longer to convince than the others, but eventually Troy had gotten through to him. His knuckles ached a bit with the old memory.

"What does this Jasper Whitlaw want?" Troy asked.

The man had had years to come looking for the child he'd left in a grocery store. Why come back for her now, when she was an adult? When she was a Colton?

She shrugged. "I don't know."

"What did he ask you for?" Troy asked. The guy had to have a reason for showing up now after all these years. He had to want something.

"He said that he just wants me to give him a call when I'm ready to talk to him."

"So he just wants to talk?" Troy asked. He didn't believe that for a minute. *Believe* was the Colton family motto, but it wasn't his, especially not after someone had broken into her cabin the day before.

Lakin nodded. "That's why he wrote his number on the back of the photograph and gave it to me," she said.

Troy wanted to wad up the picture for some reason, and he wasn't sure why. But something didn't feel right about this. Maybe the timing.

"Do you think he's the person who broke in here yesterday?" Troy asked.

She gasped. "Why would he do that? I doubt he needs food that desperately."

The man in the picture looked hungry to Troy. Of course a lot could have changed since then. It occurred to Troy that the stolen food could have been a misdirection, someone wanting the break-in to look more innocent than it was.

"I don't like this," Troy admitted. "I don't think you should call him."

"Why not?" she asked.

"I don't think you should trust him," Troy said. "I think he's after something."

"What?" she asked.

"Colton money."

She stepped back and shook her head. "*You* are the one who is obsessed with money."

"What? I don't want any Colton money," he assured her. He wanted desperately to pay his own way and hers; that was why he wanted to wait to propose and start their business until he had more money saved.

She flinched as if he'd slapped her and said, "But I'm a Colton."

He moved closer to her and gently touched his fingertips to her cheek. "Yes, you are, and I don't want your money."

"If we were really a couple, it would be *our* money," she said. She stepped back again so that his hand fell to his side.

"We are really a couple," he said, but he felt the same panic from when he'd finally realized why she was mad at him. And that she had every reason to be.

"No, we're not. You would have called me when you got hurt. You would have wanted me there for you, to support you, to comfort you."

"Lakin…" Troy didn't know what to say or how to make it up to her. He had wanted her there, but he'd been so afraid that the paralysis wouldn't go away. He hadn't wanted to stick her with someone as helpless and hopeless as he'd felt those weeks in the hospital bed.

Clearly she wasn't interested in hearing his excuses. She took the photo back from him. "But this isn't about money to me. It's about information."

"What kind of information?" he asked.

"I should know about my heritage, my genetics, what medical conditions I might pass onto kids someday." She looked up at him, her dark eyes intent on his face. "The kids *we* talked about having someday."

"We were kids ourselves when we talked about having kids," he murmured, thinking of all their teenage dreams. But then his dad had died, and Troy had been consumed with grim reality rather than dreams.

"Did you outgrow me, Troy? Our relationship? Do you want different things now?" she asked, her voice cracking slightly with emotion.

He wanted the same things he always had. A life with *her*. But if his back got screwed up again… He didn't want her to wind up like his mother, raising kids alone, struggling to make ends meet, crying from the stress after she thought they were all asleep.

"I can't think about the future right now," he said. "Not until I know how completely I'm going to heal." He was starting physical therapy soon. How his body reacted to that would determine if he would be able to go back to work on the oil rigs. Or anywhere…

"It doesn't matter to me how badly you're hurt," she said. "If you'd stayed paralyzed, it would have changed nothing for me. I love you."

"You're being naive, Lakin," he said. "It would have changed everything."

"Not my love," she said. "But apparently it changed yours." She stepped back again, drew in a shaky breath and pointed toward the door she'd left open when she stumbled in moments ago. "Just leave. I need some time alone."

"Lakin, I do love you," he insisted.

But she just shook her head, refusing to believe him.

He was tempted to remind her of her family motto: *believe*. She'd told him that once, but clearly she wasn't thinking like a Colton right now. Was she a Whitlaw? Or was this Jasper person running some scam on her?

"Please, let me be here for you," he said. He had a horrible feeling she was in danger.

"Why?" she asked. "You didn't let me be there for you. Go." She didn't wait for him to leave before she went into her bedroom like she had the night before. And like the night before, she closed and locked that door, shutting him out like she must feel he'd shut her out.

Their future was in danger, but not for the reason he'd believed—not because of his injury but because of him.

Why couldn't she see that he'd been thinking about her, that he hadn't wanted her to make any sacrifices for him? He loved her so much that he wanted all her dreams to come true.

Even if those dreams no longer included him.

The hook was baited. Now the fisherman just had to wait for the right moment to reel her in.

Then, finally, after all these years of planning, he could be certain this part of his life was over.

And so was hers...

## Chapter 7

Once the door to the cabin closed behind Troy, Lakin left her bedroom and went into the RTA office. She spent the day there, doing what she always did: taking calls, talking to clients and vendors, putting out little fires. And yet she felt like it wasn't real, like she was in a *Groundhog Day*-like dream. She was doing the same thing over and over, but she wasn't really present.

She wasn't sure where she was, but she knew where she wanted to be. And once she left the office, she hopped in her SUV and headed there. Home.

Not to her empty cabin but to the house where she'd grown up with her brothers and her mom and dad.

Because it was home and would always be, she didn't knock. She just pushed open the kitchen door and walked in, surprising her parents at the counter. Her dad had his arms around her mom as she was chopping up something on the cutting board, and he was nuzzling her neck as she squirmed and giggled.

Lakin's heart warmed with love for them and for

the love that they had for each other all these years later. They'd been high school sweethearts like her and Troy, but unlike her and Troy, they'd shared their vision for family and their future.

And their love thrived even or maybe especially during the tragedies they'd suffered.

"Oh, there's our baby girl!" Mom exclaimed as she dropped the knife and rushed over to hug Lakin.

Lakin smiled over being called baby. She was taller and bigger boned than her mother. Sasha Colton had a delicate build and facial features, but she was strong and fiercely loving and fun. She had so many friends because everyone who met her became her friend.

What about…? The woman in the photograph suddenly popped into Lakin's head, the woman who'd looked so much like her. She felt a twinge of guilt.

Sasha Colton was the woman who'd raised her, who'd read to her at night and helped her with homework and talked to her about friends and boys and life.

Lakin tightened her arms around her mother, holding tight to her for a moment and to those memories. She breathed in the scents in the kitchen. The roasting chicken. The cinnamon and nutmeg spices from the Dutch apple pie cooling on the counter. And her mother's hair brushed across her cheek, soft and smelling like a combination of the cooking aromas, spring and clay.

She smiled again. "I love you so much, Mom," she said.

Sasha clasped her tightly. She was as famous for her hugs as for her pottery and her cooking. "I love you, too, baby."

"What about me?" her dad asked.

Lakin and her mother laughed. "Of course we love you, too," they said together.

When they stepped back from each other, her dad hugged Lakin. Almost too tightly, like he was trying too hard to hang onto her.

Did he know about Jasper Whitlaw's visit? Had Troy told him? He might have out of concern, but then he should have been concerned that he would make her even more mad at him. She doubted he would risk that.

Maybe Eli or Kansas had told Dad about the break-in at the cabin last night. But she didn't think either of them would want to worry him when they'd really seemed to believe it was just a hungry vagrant.

But was that really the case? While she hadn't felt that strange sensation of being watched since this morning, she felt it now. Was it because of how intently her parents were staring at her or...

Was there someone outside watching?

She glanced through the front windows of the house and noted a few trucks and other vehicles parked on the street. With the sun shining on the windows, she couldn't see inside them. Maybe they weren't all empty. Maybe someone was out there peering back at her. Whitlaw? Or someone else?

Once her dad released her, she walked over to the window and closed the blinds.

"Too bright?" Sasha asked.

Lakin nodded. The truth was she wanted to shield her parents from that watchful gaze. She wanted to protect them. So she couldn't tell them about Jasper Whitlaw and that photograph. She knew they would seek him out and try to get answers for her like they'd tried all those years ago. For some reason, she didn't want them anywhere near Whitlaw or her long-ago past.

After they adopted her, the Coltons had given her such a wonderful, perfect childhood. Even though she was an adult now, they were still here for her, helping her make her dreams come true. If she hadn't reached out to her father during that auction for the Shelby hotel, she would have lost her opportunity for the business she always wanted. But, despite what Troy believed, the money wasn't as important as the fact that her dad believed in her.

He and her mother always had.

"I don't know if I tell you enough how much I love you two," Lakin said.

Her mom smiled. "You definitely tell us enough, but I love hearing it." She hugged Lakin again. "And I hope you know how much we love you."

"I have never doubted your love," she assured them.

"Uh-oh," her dad murmured.

"What?" her mom asked with a glance at him.

"I feel like there is a story behind that statement," he said. "Trouble with Troy? I know he's been gone a long time…"

"He's back," Lakin said.

Her dad arched an eyebrow. "And you're here without him?"

She nodded. "I need some space," she admitted.

"Uh-oh," her father said again.

Tears rushed to her eyes, but she blinked them away. She didn't want to start crying because she was afraid she might not stop. "Can we talk about that later?" she asked.

She had to figure out first if she could just be happy that Troy was okay and not worry about how he hadn't called anyone when he got hurt or how uncertain he was about the future. She wanted to be understanding, but she'd been patient so long with him. She wasn't sure she had any patience left.

"Of course," her mom said. Then she turned toward her husband and gave him a pointed look. "We're not going to pry, are we, Will?"

He sighed. "No, we're not."

Lakin smiled in appreciation; she knew how hard it was for him to not step in and help her. Ever since they brought her home, her father and brothers had been the white knights trying to slay her dragons. Mom had always been the one encouraging her to slay her own dragons and having the faith in her that she had the strength to do that.

But now her mom's face flushed a bit and she murmured, "We were actually going to call you about moving back home for a while."

Lakin groaned. "Eli told you?"

"About that girl's body being found," her dad said with a nod. "Yes. And I know you probably think we're being overly cautious, but you shouldn't be alone in your cabin. It's too far from the other guest cottages."

It didn't sound to Lakin like they knew about the break-in the day before. That was good. It was also the least of the things she was keeping from them right now. But she didn't want to worry them any more than they already were.

"And you said you want some space from Troy, so you really will be alone out there," her dad added.

"Troy spent last night on the couch," she admitted,

Her mom smiled. "Of course he would be worried, too, and want to protect you. He loves you so much."

Lakin sighed. "I'm not so sure about that anymore." Did he really love her, or was he just used to protecting her and everyone else in his family? He probably believed that he'd been protecting them when he didn't call after his fall.

"What happened?" her dad asked, his long body stiffening with outrage. Like he intended to go defend her honor.

Tears sprang to her eyes again, blurring her vision for a moment. He was her father no matter what Jasper Whitlaw claimed he was; he hadn't been there for her like Will Colton had always been.

"I don't want to pry, honey," her mom said as she slid her arm around her shoulders. "But you seem really upset, and you might feel better if you talk about it."

"Troy got hurt…" her voice cracked "…badly on the oil rig."

Her mother gasped. "Is he all right?"

Lakin nodded. "Now. And I am relieved and grateful that he is." If he hadn't recovered… She couldn't even consider the horror of that without more tears rushing to her eyes.

"But?" her mother prodded.

"But he was in the hospital for weeks, and he didn't call me," she said. "He didn't let me know."

"He probably didn't want to worry you," her dad said.

"He still should have called," her mom said. "Men and their foolish pride, trying so hard to be strong for us." The look she gave her husband was telling.

Lakin understood. These killings had to have brought back all the pain of his family tragedy, the loss of his parents and sister. She hugged him.

Her father patted her back, comforting her instead of accepting her comfort. "You and Troy will work this out," he said. "I don't remember a time that you weren't in love with him and he with you."

Neither did Lakin. She'd loved him for so long. But she sighed again. "I don't know if we want the same things anymore," she explained. She wanted it all, the business, kids, a family...

"Oh," Mom said, her brow furrowing beneath a lock of silvery gray hair. "That's hard."

It was. But so was this, being here with her parents and keeping so much from them. Lakin wanted to tell them both everything like she always had. But she didn't want to worry them. Like Troy hadn't wanted to worry her...

Maybe she was a hypocrite to be mad at him for doing what she was doing. While she could forgive him for not telling her about his accident right away, she wasn't sure if she could continue on the way that they'd been for so long, this long-distance limbo waiting for their future together to start.

Life was too short for that, as his accident should have made him realize. As the horrible deaths of those women had made her realize.

"Well, dinner is almost ready," her mom said. "I hope you're hungry."

Despite the delicious smells, Lakin's stomach churned at the thought of food. She shook her head. "I had a late lunch. I didn't stop in for dinner, just to check on you two."

"We're fine," her dad said. "But we would be better if you'd stay with us."

She smiled at his not-so-subtle manipulation. "I will be fine in my cabin. Like I told Troy, I need some time alone."

"Right now isn't the safest time to be alone," her father persisted.

She sighed. "I promise I'll be fine." She hugged them both again. "Love you, and I will see you later."

As she left, she couldn't help but feel like she shouldn't have come at all. That she'd brought whoever was watching her to the loving home that Will and Sasha Colton had made for Lakin and her brothers.

She wanted that person, that stalker, to leave with her; she didn't want whatever was going on with her to touch her family or hurt them in any way.

Troy felt like a stalker. He'd been following Lakin around all day, sitting in his truck, keeping an eye on her, making sure that nothing and nobody threatened her. So it was kind of ironic when he received a threat.

It was a call from his supervisor. Troy answered it, thinking the man was just calling to check up on him, not so much because he cared about his health but because he wanted him back on the job.

"What the hell are you thinking, Amos?"

"What do you mean?" Troy asked. "You know I'm not cleared yet to return to work."

"So you're suing the company? You're not going to win. In fact you're going to lose big and probably more than just your job."

"What do you mean?" Troy repeated. More than just his job? What else could his employer take from him?

But Harrison didn't answer him, just disconnected the call.

"What the hell was that about?"

Troy texted Mitch: I take it you contacted the oil company. I just got an interesting call.

Mitch texted back: Don't talk to them again. Let me handle everything.

Gladly.

The last thing Troy wanted to deal with was work when he was home. He didn't even want to think about it. He wanted to focus only on Lakin, especially now with that weird man accosting her and claiming to be her father.

And the break-in...

They had to be related, more so than she probably was to the man. But the woman in the picture was clearly her biological mother, so he understood why she'd been so shaken. And why she would want to learn more.

He just didn't want anyone hurting her. Not Jasper Whitlaw, not her biological mother, the intruder, that serial killer or even himself.

But it was too late for him. He'd already hurt her. Now he had to do everything he could to make it up to her. Like keeping her safe.

However, after an uneventful day sitting outside the RTA office, he'd begun to think he was just paranoid.

But when she drove from the office to her parents'

house, he wasn't the only one following her. Another truck was between his SUV and hers. It followed every turn she made. When she parked in her parents' driveway, the truck pulled up to the curb across the street from her childhood home.

Somebody was following her. Someone besides him.

Troy wanted that person to know he'd seen them. He edged away from the curb and started down the street to where they'd parked. He wanted to see who this person was. He wanted to know who was following Lakin.

But when he got close to the truck, the old vehicle pulled away from the curb and sped off down the street. Undeterred, Troy followed.

Despite its rusty condition and worn-looking tires, the truck was fast. Puffs of black smoke from the exhaust clouded Troy's vision, so he couldn't see the license plate nor could he tell what make or model it was. He pressed harder on the accelerator and held tight to the steering wheel as they rounded the road's sharp curves out of town, toward the mountains.

The driver had to know the area or was just a damn good driver. They barely kicked up any gravel on the side of the road whereas Troy's tires dropped off the asphalt a few times and spewed gravel up behind him. He eased up on the accelerator, slowing down for the next sharp curve. But when he rounded it, he didn't see any sign of the truck he'd been following.

Had it gotten that far ahead of him?

He continued on, driving more slowly, checking the side of the road. But as the road wound higher into the mountains, there was less room on either side. On the right was the side of mountain; on the left, a steep drop.

"Where did you go?" Troy muttered. He came around another curve, and there it was, in the center of the road, blocking his way.

He tapped his brakes and tightened his grasp on the steering wheel, swerving so he wouldn't hit the rusted-out truck. His tires dropped off the asphalt, sending gravel and rocks tumbling down the side of the mountain. He jerked the wheel the other way, trying to correct, trying to stop himself from driving right off the mountain.

But it was too late.

After learning that the serial killer had claimed another victim, Will had been anxious to see Lakin and make sure that she was all right. But her visit hadn't reassured him at all.

"She'll be okay," Sasha assured him. "Our little girl is tough."

Abandoned at three, she'd had to be tough, but she'd never gotten bitter or resentful. She was such a loving, forgiving person. So beautiful outside and in, like Caroline.

His niece, Kansas, looked more like his late little sister, but something about Lakin reminded him more of the girl who'd never aged beyond seventeen because of an obsessed stalker. Caroline had drawn people to her with her beauty and her spirit, and Lakin had that same spirit. Her smile lit up a room. He remembered the first time they'd seen her, and his boys, older than her and rough-and-tumble, had been immediately drawn to her. They'd fallen for her as hard as he and Sasha had.

As hard as Troy Amos had.

He sighed. "I would feel better if Troy was staying with her."

"He did last night, and even though Lakin wants some space, he won't be far away from her," Sasha said. "Troy Amos is proud, but the man is no fool. He knows Lakin is the love of his life."

"As he is hers," Will said. "It's so hard to see any of our kids hurting."

"She's tough," Sasha repeated. "She'll survive some heartache."

"Do you think that's all that was bothering her?" Will asked.

"You don't?"

He shook his head. He knew their little girl well. "She got out of here fast, and closing the blinds…"

"You think she's worried someone was watching her?" Sasha asked, her blue eyes widening with alarm.

His blood chilled at the thought that someone could be watching Lakin like someone had been watching Caroline all those years ago. Back then the authorities, and even their parents, hadn't believed that Caroline's *fan* was actually dangerous.

Jason Stevens had proved how dangerous he was.

If someone was watching Lakin, hopefully they weren't a killer.

# Chapter 8

The minute Lakin stepped out of her parents' house, she'd noticed the trucks speeding off down the road. They were both old, one more rusted than the other. The less rusted one showed traces of teal blue paint, and there was a shiny chrome toolbox in the bed of the truck.

"Troy…"

Was he the one who'd been watching her? But his gaze had never creeped her out; it had always warmed her with love and desire, somehow both reassuring and exciting. And he'd just returned to Shelby, so there was no way he was the one who'd been watching her over the past couple of weeks.

Had that been Jasper Whitlaw? Was that who Troy had sped after? Or was it someone else in the other vehicle?

Anxious to find out what was going on, she hopped into her SUV and headed after the two trucks.

She wasn't brave enough to drive as fast as they were around those sharp curves. The road was too narrow the higher it wound up the mountain, leaving rock on one side and nothingness on the other. She didn't bother trying to call or text Troy. She didn't want to be distracted and she didn't want to distract him from whatever he was doing.

A high-speed chase up a mountain? Who was he so intent on catching that he was risking his life? And this after he'd had such a close call falling off the oil rig. She shuddered as fear gripped her.

"Stop!" she called out, wishing he could hear her. They were going so fast, though, that she quickly lost sight of them. She slowed down, peering off the side and around the curves ahead.

A truck nearly sideswiped her as it raced past. It was so fast that she couldn't see the driver nor the vehicle itself clearly. She jerked her wheel toward the right and nearly struck rock. When she pulled back to the left, she glanced in her rearview mirror. The truck gave a quick flash of brake lights as it slowed. But it didn't stop and soon disappeared from view.

Where was Troy? Why was the one vehicle heading back down, but he wasn't following it?

"Troy?" she called out as if he could hear her. But then she heard the sound of another motor. Smoke was billowing from an exhaust pipe sticking up from the side of the road. That and a rear bumper were all she could see. Troy's truck.

She braked, engaged the hazard lights and jumped out and raced across the road. Her heart pounded with fear that she was too late.

And she'd been such a bitch to him.

Sure, he hadn't called when he got hurt, but he'd been hurt. And scared. And sure, he hadn't reached out to her, but it hadn't been about her. Since he'd come home, she'd made it all about her. No wonder he hadn't reached out when he was hurt; he hadn't wanted to comfort her or focus on her. He'd wanted to focus on healing.

If he was hurt again, he might have undone all that healing. How hard it must be for him to have to live with the fear that paralysis could return if he wasn't careful.

"Troy!" she yelled.

The rear tires of the truck spun, gravel flying as he tried to back up, but the truck didn't move backward. Instead it slipped a few more inches forward, over the steep incline of rock and gravel that made up the side of the mountain.

"Troy! Get out!" she yelled over the roar of the engine he was gunning. The truck was going to go over the steep side with him in it. This would not be a fall that either his truck or he would survive. "Troy!"

He must have heard her or seen her in the side mirror because he rolled down his window. "Get out of here, Lakin! You're going to get hurt."

"No. You get out of there!" she shouted back. "Jump out before it goes over!"

But he kept spinning his back wheels, spewing more gravel. Yet again, instead of going backward, the truck slipped forward a bit more.

"Get out!" she yelled again.

"If I take my foot off the gas, it's going over," he told her as he kept gunning the engine.

Her heart pounded hard. "What can I do?" She'd left her phone in her purse. But if she ran to get it and the truck went over... Tears burned her eyes. "I love you," she said.

"What the hell are you two doing?" a voice asked, the words slightly slurred.

Lakin glanced behind her to see Billy Hoover hanging out the side window of his truck, staring down at them. "Billy!" Was his the truck that had nearly run her off the road and probably Troy as well?

"Do you have a tow strap?" Troy yelled out his window.

Billy nodded, then pushed his greasy red hair out of his face.

"Hurry!" Lakin said. At the moment she was less concerned that Billy might have caused the crash than she was about making him help rescue the man she loved.

She was the one who wrapped the tow strap around Troy's hitch and then Billy's, making sure both ends were secure. Billy didn't even get out of his truck, but that was fine.

"Gun it!" she yelled at them both.

Gravel flew and metal crunched as Troy's truck came up the side of the mountain and bounced back onto the road, colliding with the back bumper of Billy's truck as the redhaired man abruptly stopped.

Troy hopped out of his truck. Lakin would have

rushed to hug him, but her legs were shaking too badly. She couldn't get over how close she'd come to losing him forever. If that truck had gone over… She glimpsed over the steep drop. There was no way he would have survived that fall.

"You're going to have to pay for that, Amos," Billy shouted over his loud motor.

"Like you can tell what damage my truck did to yours," Troy remarked as he unwound the strap from his hitch.

Before he could take it off Billy's, the other man sped away, the strap trailing behind him. The dents and dings on Billy's rusted truck were undoubtedly caused by how the man drove. Despite his help, Lakin was tempted to call the police. Billy had obviously been drinking. And if he'd caused the crash, she would.

"What happened?" Lakin asked Troy, her heart still pounding frantically even though he was back on solid ground. She wanted to run and hug him even now, but she wasn't sure her legs would hold her up.

He leaned against the side of his truck still idling in the road near hers. Maybe he was as shaken as she was. "Someone ran me off the road."

"Was it Billy?" she asked.

He glanced in the direction their old school nemesis had gone. "I don't know for sure. It was a rusted truck, too, but I didn't get a good look at it or the driver."

Could it be Billy who was watching her? She

hadn't considered it, but he'd been a bully as a child. What could he be now? A stalker? A serial killer?

She shivered as she had that sensation again that someone was watching her. Watching both of them now, and maybe getting ready to try something... while she and Troy were just standing in the road, both easy targets.

"Let's get out of here," Troy said, and he levered himself away from the side of his pickup. "It's not safe standing in the road or even parked alongside it. Get in your vehicle, too, and let's head back to your cabin."

Lakin didn't argue with him. He could have died if Billy hadn't come along when he had. Even though Troy hadn't been able to see who'd forced him off the road, they needed to call the police. She would insist that they did.

Later. When they were safe...

Instead of locking him out, Lakin held open the door for him when Troy walked up to her cabin. Or limped, actually. He tried not to grimace as he climbed the couple of steps and crossed the porch to her.

Going off the road had jarred his back again. Maybe it had already been hurting from taking the turns as fast as he had. And then Billy Hoover jerking the truck up the embankment with the tow strap hadn't helped, either, but it had kept the truck and Troy from sliding down the mountain.

Was Billy the one who'd driven him off in the first place though? If so, from how he'd slurred his words, it might not have been intentional. Either way Troy should have called the police, but he'd wanted to make sure that Lakin was somewhere safe first.

Once he hobbled inside her cabin, he closed and dead-bolted her door. He wasn't sure even that would be enough to keep them safe if someone was really determined to hurt them, though.

Her?

Or him? His supervisor's words echoed inside his head. He might lose more than his job? His life? Or the woman who was the most important part of his life?

Lakin threw her arms around his neck and pressed her body against his. She was trembling. "I was so scared," she said. "I thought I was going to lose you."

He closed his arms around her and held her tightly against him. God, he'd missed her so damn much. Not just the weeks he'd been gone, but since he'd been back there'd been such a distance between them. He tipped her face up to his and lowered his mouth, brushing it across her lips.

Her breath whispered out, heating his skin, making him tingle. He wanted to deepen the kiss, but she stepped back and dropped her arms from around him.

"Why are you following me?" Lakin asked.

"I wanted to make sure you got safely home," he explained. Her safety was what mattered most to him.

"I mean earlier," she said. "I know you were parked outside my parents' house. I saw your truck pull away when I walked outside. Why were you there?"

He sighed and pushed his hand through his hair. "I don't like that after all these years some guy shows up claiming to be your father and that he approached you right after someone broke in here."

"For food."

"You don't know that's really why they broke in," he pointed out. "Because of the break-in and how shaken you were after Whitlaw came up to you, I wanted to keep an eye on you." He wanted more than his eye on her, but she'd put distance between them again. "And I don't think I was the only one following you."

She shivered but didn't argue with him. And she didn't seem at all surprised, either.

"You know someone's been following you," he surmised.

She shrugged. "I don't know for sure. I've never seen anyone. Did you get a look at this person?"

He shook his head. "When I tried, they drove off."

"And you sped off after them," she said, her breath catching. "You could have been hurt or worse, Troy. That was so dangerous."

"Yes, it was," he agreed. "This person following you is dangerous."

She closed her eyes and sighed. "I just can't be certain someone really is and that it's not just paranoia about the serial killer and the other things that have happened in Shelby lately."

Maybe because he finally knew about all those dangerous occurrences, he'd assumed his supervisor's call was a threat. But it could have been empty. What had happened on the mountain could have been an accident. But he didn't really believe he was over-reacting to any of it.

"I think it's better to be safe than sorry," he said. And he would be more than sorry if something happened to Lakin; he would be devastated. "We should call the police."

Though he wasn't sure what they could do about him being run off the road. There were no cameras up in the mountains, and he wouldn't be able to give them a license plate number or even a good description.

"Bobby Reynolds was here the other night with Eli and Kansas," she reminded him. Bobby was the officer who'd been with Shelby PD the longest. "He wasn't concerned about the break-in here at the cabin."

"I'm concerned," Troy said. "About the break-in. About this man claiming to be your father. And who-ever's following you…" He wasn't just concerned; he was scared to death that something was going to happen to her. "Is there anything else you haven't told me?"

Her dark eyes widened for a moment, and her mouth opened. Finally she said, "Yes."

He gasped. "What?" Had something else horrible happened?

"When you didn't reply to my emails and texts about the Shelby Hotel, I went to the auction anyway," she said. Then she paused, drew in a deep breath and said, "And I bought it."

"What?" That was not what he'd expected her to say. It had nothing to do with the break-in and Whitlaw. "I don't understand."

"I bought the Shelby Hotel," she said. "I actually got a great deal on it."

"But the auction meant you had to pay cash. No matter how great a deal, how would you have enough cash to purchase it?" he asked.

Her face flushed slightly, and she glanced down. "My dad helped me."

Her dad had helped her because Troy wouldn't. He hadn't seen her texts or emails until after he'd recovered in the hospital. But even if he had seen them before the auction, he wasn't sure he would have been able to help her no matter how cheap the hotel had sold.

"I'm going to pay him back," Lakin said. "I'm working on getting a business loan now for that and for renovations and carrying costs. I have a plan."

"I…" It used to be *we. We had a plan.*

"I got sick of waiting for our future to start, Troy," she said. "I love the idea of turning the old hotel into an experience with gorgeous suites for guests to celebrate their special occasions, like honeymoons and anniversaries."

"The renovations are going to take a lot of money," he said.

He'd driven past it earlier when he'd followed her to her parents' house. Because she'd slowed down as she'd passed it, he had, too. And he'd really studied the place. The wood siding was weathered, and while he hadn't been able to see the roof of the two-story building, he was worried that it probably needed to be replaced, too. If the roof had been leaking, there would be a lot of renovations required inside, too.

"And it's going to take a lot of hard work, too, to get it up and running," he said. He wasn't really capable of the hard work, not yet. And the money. He'd already lost too many weeks' wages, and if he lost his job, too, now, there was no way he could help her with anything.

She nodded. "Yes, I know all that, and I'm willing to do the hard work."

"You have a job." One that he thought she'd enjoyed since she was working with her family.

"I'm going to give Parker my notice soon, once the business loan is approved," she said.

"You've made a lot of decisions while I was gone," he said. He felt left behind and left out, like he was still stuck in that hospital bed, paralyzed while she was running circles around him.

"I tried to get in contact with you—"

"I was in the hospital!" he said, his voice a bit

sharp. He would have answered his emails or texts. But his phone had gone in the water with him, and he hadn't been able to replace it until he'd gotten better.

"I didn't know that," she said, "because you didn't *let* me know that." The hurt was in her voice and in the depths of her dark eyes.

He released a ragged sigh. "I'm sorry," he said, and he stepped closer to her. "I never meant to hurt you. I was trying to spare you…"

"What? All the fear you must have been feeling?" she asked. "You should not have had to go through that alone, but you chose to. And I don't understand why."

"You don't?" he asked. "You're clearly not eager to call the police about someone following you, about Whitlaw…"

"I don't know that there is anything to tell," she said. "You have more to report with someone running you off the road."

"I'll go by the police department tomorrow," he said. "And you should go with me."

"I'll talk to Eli," she said. "I don't want it getting around town about Whitlaw."

"So you didn't tell your parents about him and the photograph he gave you," he surmised.

She sighed. "No. I didn't want to worry them."

He touched her chin, tipping it up to him. "Why not? Because you love them? I love you, Lakin. That's why I didn't want to worry you."

"It's not just your accident, though," she said.

"You're gone so much, and I hear so little from you when you're on the rig."

They were drifting apart. He hadn't realized how much until now.

"Lakin, what's going on with us?" Their relationship had always been so loving and easy. Until now. And he didn't know how to fix it.

She shrugged. "I don't know. We just don't feel like us anymore. Maybe our lives aren't going in the same direction anymore."

"I love you," he repeated, trying to get through to her that he hadn't changed and that his feelings hadn't changed. When she'd been angry with him earlier about not calling her after his accident, she'd doubted his love.

"And I love you," she said, but she sounded more resigned than happy about it.

Until now, he'd never realized that their love might not be enough.

The truck with the rust eating away at the bright blue paint was parked outside her cabin next to her SUV. It should have gone over the side of the mountain with the man inside it. He should have died.

While he'd survived this time, the boyfriend had to go. He was a pain in the ass, and he was going to get in the way and mess up the plan.

He had to die.

# Chapter 9

Lakin saw the hurt and the fear on Troy's face after her declaration of love. She knew he was thinking the same thing she was, that it wasn't enough. They were slipping away from each other.

Earlier tonight, he'd nearly slipped over the side of a mountain. He could have been lost to her forever. She wanted to hang onto him like she had when he walked into the cabin earlier. Like she had every other time he'd come home after a long time away from her. She wasn't thinking about the space that she'd told her parents she wanted from Troy. She was thinking of having no space between them at all.

"I was so afraid when I saw your truck over the side like that..." she murmured, her voice hoarse from yelling at him and at Billy, trying to be heard over their engines.

"I'm fine," Troy said. "I'll go into the police station tomorrow and report it."

"Just that," she said. "I don't want to talk to the local police about Jasper Whitlaw." She refused to call the man her father.

"You need to talk to someone about him. Have someone check him out," Troy persisted.

"I don't want to talk at all," she said. Talking with Troy just led to frustration and disillusionment over their future. She didn't want to talk or think or worry right now. She just wanted to feel.

Him.

She stepped closer to him now and pressed her palms against the sculpted muscles of his chest. Through his T-shirt she could feel the heat of his skin and the hard beat of his heart. Then she moved her hands up over his shoulders and pulled his head down toward hers.

His beautiful green eyes darkened with the desire already burning in her. "Lakin…" he whispered, his voice sounding even more hoarse than hers.

"I need you," she said. "I need to feel that you're alive and well…that you survived…" Not just tonight but that fall as well. Every time she closed her eyes, she imagined him dropping down from the rig into the dark cold depths of the ocean. Disappearing under the water and out of her life.

"I'm alive and well," he said with a smile. "I'm also aching for you…"

He'd limped when he walked up to her cabin earlier. "I don't think you're aching for me," she said.

He took one of her hands and pulled it between their bodies. She could feel the hard ridge of his erection pressing against the fly of his jeans. "I've missed you…so damn much…"

She'd missed him as well, too much to continue to deny herself. Especially after tonight, after he could have died once again. This time, not on a rig but because he'd been trying to catch her stalker. If that was even who it was…

She closed her eyes, trying to shut out those thoughts, those fears.

And he kissed her.

His mouth moved hungrily over hers. She parted her lips, deepening the kiss. As they kissed, they moved together toward the open door to her bedroom. But it was like a slow dance, not the usual frenzy when they first saw each other after a long separation.

Troy didn't pick her up and carry her to the bed. Instead he moved stiffly, walking with her through her bedroom door toward her bed. When they got near it, they fell down onto the comforter. She felt Troy grimace and heard his sharp intake of breath.

She pulled back, panting for air herself, and asked, "Are you okay?"

He nodded, but his jaw was clenched like he was gritting his teeth. Was he in pain?

"Can you do this?" she asked. "Or will this hurt you more?"

"It'll hurt me more to not be with you," he said. "I have been aching for you, Lakin. To kiss you, to touch you…" And he kissed her again.

Then he began to undress her. Every inch of skin he uncovered, he caressed and kissed. He glided his mouth over her shoulder and then along the ridge of her collarbone and down to her breasts. As he drew one nipple into his mouth, he stroked the other with his thumb.

She was the one hurting now, her body tense and needy for his. She tried to touch him, too, but gently, so she wouldn't hurt him.

But he was so focused on her. He moved his head from her breasts over her stomach to her core. And he made love to her with his mouth. As he did, she came, crying out softly with the pleasure and the release flowing through her.

But it wasn't enough. He wasn't close enough.

"Please," she murmured. "I need you."

"*I* need *you*."

But he hadn't. When it counted most, he'd shut her out. She tried to shut that thought off, push it out of her mind. She focused only on him, gliding her hands and mouth over his muscled chest and arms.

It was as if their clothes had dissolved. She'd barely noticed him undressing himself. But now she took advantage of his nakedness and wrapped her hand around his pulsating erection.

He sucked in a breath, then he moved between her legs. She guided him inside her, arching to take him deeper. He moved slowly; she wasn't sure if it was because of the injury to his back or because he wanted to drive her out of her mind. The slow strokes built the tension inside her again, and she arched and writhed, moving faster.

Then he reached between their bodies and stroked the most sensitive part of her. She came, yelling his name. Then he tensed again, and at first she thought he was hurt because of the grimace on his face. Then his body shuddered, and he filled her with his release.

While they'd made love with all their normal passion, she didn't feel as close to him as she usually felt. The distance remained between them.

If love couldn't bridge it, she wasn't sure what could.

Even though they'd made love the night before, Troy knew he was losing Lakin. And not just because she was gone when he woke up. He wasn't even sure if she slept beside him last night.

After he dressed, he went out into the living room and saw her pillow on the couch with a throw blanket. Sometime during the night, she'd left her bed. She'd wanted physical distance between them again.

But she shouldn't have gone off alone, not with a serial killer on the loose. And whatever Whitlaw really was to her... Father? Intruder? Stalker? Troy had no idea, but he needed to find out.

Yet, when he went to the police department to report the incident on the road last night, he didn't mention Whitlaw at all. Last night Lakin had told him not to, and when he'd stopped at the RTA office to make sure she wasn't alone, she'd reminded him in a whisper to not mention it, that she was going to talk to Eli.

That was good. But she needed to do it soon.

At least she was safe at the office with Parker and Spence both there. So Troy would go to his first physical therapy session once Officer Reynolds finished taking his report.

"Billy Hoover filed one earlier this morning," Reynolds remarked.

"He admitted to running me off the road?" Troy asked with surprise.

Reynolds shook his head. "He said you were already off the road when he rescued you, and that for his trouble, you damaged his truck and ruined his tow strap. He figures you must have been drunk."

Troy gasped at the outrageous claim.

Reynolds chuckled. "Yeah, I pointed out that it was too late for me to tell now and that you both should have called me to the scene. I know why he didn't." Obviously the officer knew who'd really been drunk. "But why didn't you?"

"Lakin was with me, and it was getting late. After getting run off the road once, I didn't want to risk it happening again." Troy didn't want her to be in any danger. Although until that serial killer was caught, everybody was.

Reynolds nodded. "Yeah, everybody needs to be extra vigilant right now. Keep an eye out for anything strange."

"I wish I'd gotten a better look at the truck and the driver that did cause me to go off the road."

"Me, too. That road is too dangerous for anyone to be driving that recklessly."

Troy's face heated a bit. He'd been driving reck-lessly himself to try to catch the guy. "I thought he might have been following Lakin, that he might be who broke into her cabin the night before that."

Reynolds sighed. "That was probably just a va-grant or a teenager looking for alcohol and made off with some food instead."

"I hope you're right." But Troy didn't really believe that he was. Or that he would find the intruder at all. Hopefully Lakin would talk to Eli soon.

The officer passed a card across the desk to him. "Here's your report number if you need it for insurance."

"Thanks." Troy didn't have full coverage, so he wouldn't be filing a claim. But it made him think of the workers compensation and disability suit Mitch was filing for him to get back some of his lost wages and to make sure his medical bills were covered.

But it wasn't just the money he was concerned about replacing now. He didn't want to lose his job or whatever else his supervisor had so very vaguely threatened. When Troy was done with his physical therapy session, he would drop by Mitch's law office.

As he left the police station, Troy had that strange sensation that Lakin had mentioned the night before, as if someone was watching him.

Who?

And why?

Mitch's lips still tingled from Dove's kiss even though she'd left his office a while ago. He'd never felt like this before and wouldn't have believed he ever would, especially with someone as totally different from him as Dove St. James. But maybe that was what made her so damn exciting.

"You look happy," a deep voice remarked.

"I am," Mitch said, and he looked up from his desk to see Troy Amos walking into his office. Limping actually. The man was obviously in pain. Mitch jumped up. "You okay? Need anything?"

Troy shook his head and grimaced. "First physical therapy session."

"Hope you didn't overdo it," Mitch said.

"I've got to get back to work," Troy said. "But it sounds like I may not have a job to go back to."

"That's illegal for them to threaten your employment over a work comp claim," Mitch said. "It's only going to make our case stronger."

"I'm not sure my job is all he threatened," Troy said.

Mitch tensed. "I have been hearing some things," he admitted.

"Like what?"

"Like this oil company doesn't like to pay out for anything."

"I figured that out already," Troy said with a slight grin.

But it had to be frustrating for Troy with all the years he and his father had worked for this company. "I'm going to make sure that they do this time, no matter what," Mitch said. "But be careful."

In a lot of lawsuits against this company, the plaintiffs had withdrawn their claims. Mitch wondered now if they'd been threatened into doing that.

Troy nodded. "I will. But I'm not as worried about me as I am Lakin."

"You think they'll go after her?" Mitch asked with alarm.

"I really don't think they'll go after either of us," Troy said. "Now that I've had some time to think about it, I think Harrison was probably as drunk as Billy Hoover was last night. He's probably the one who's going to end up fired."

Mitch nodded. "Supervisor on the job site. He probably will be sacrificed as the scapegoat."

"He should have made sure the equipment was in better condition," Troy said. "But I didn't intend for him to lose his job."

"We'll see what happens," Mitch said. But he was definitely going to add some things to the lawsuit to put the pressure on the defendants to settle quickly.

"Thanks for taking this on for me," Troy said.

"Of course."

Troy started turning toward the door, but Mitch stopped him. "If you're not worried about the oil company coming after Lakin, why are you worried about her?" He loved his little sister so much, but he'd been so busy that he hadn't seen much of her lately.

Troy lifted his shoulders in a slight shrug. "I guess I'm just worried because of everything that's been happening in Shelby."

"The serial killer," Mitch said, and his stomach tightened into knots of tension and dread. "We're all worried about that." The murderer needed to be caught before he hurt anyone else. He had faith that his older brother would catch the killer.

Troy nodded. "Yeah…"

"Yeah?" Was that really the reason?

But Troy slipped out of the office before Mitch could question him further.

And the lawyer wondered. Was there another reason that Troy was worried about Lakin? Another reason that meant Mitch should be worried about her, too?

# Chapter 10

A few days had passed since Jasper Whitlaw had given Lakin the photograph that she stared at while sitting at her desk in the RTA office. She hadn't told anyone but Troy about it yet. He'd wanted to bring Jasper Whitlaw up to Bobby Reynolds, but she'd made Troy promise to keep all of that quiet until she found a way to tell her parents.

Lakin didn't want to upset them more than they already were about the recent murders. They were already worried enough about her. They kept calling to try to get her to stay with them. But after knowing that someone had probably followed her to their house the other night, she was determined to stay away. She didn't want to put either of them in danger if she was.

But why would she be? It didn't make any sense that someone would want to hurt her. Or want anything from her.

What did Jasper Whitlaw want?

Troy was convinced that the man had an agenda for seeking her out. He was even more worried about her than her parents were. He'd insisted on staying with her, but he'd moved back to the couch, telling her that he didn't want to chase her from her own bed like he had the other night. After they'd made love...

That had been a mistake. Making love with him again hadn't brought her closer to him but had somehow highlighted the distance between them.

Usually after they made love, they would cuddle and discuss the future, making plans. But Troy clearly didn't want to talk about the future at all.

Maybe that was just because of the uncertainty over his injury. But he was going to physical therapy; he seemed to be getting better. Still, he didn't talk to her about the hotel or ask if she'd gotten the business loan yet. He didn't seem any more interested in their future than in getting back into her bed.

Maybe he'd thought it was a mistake, too. And maybe not just making love but their whole relationship.

She wasn't sure now if they had a future together. The doubts churned in her stomach, making her queasy despite the fact she hadn't even had any coffee lately. After losing her mugs off the roof of the SUV, she hadn't gone back to Roasters. She hadn't wanted to risk running into Jasper Whitlaw there again.

But when she looked up from her desk, she found him standing over her. His sudden appearance startled her for a number of reasons, not least of which was that she'd thought she was alone in the office.

Spence and Parker had left some time ago to lead hiking and fishing tours respectively. She must have been so lost in her thoughts that she hadn't noticed him open the door and walk into the building.

"So you haven't lost my number," Whitlaw remarked, his dark eyes cold as he stared down at her.

She suddenly felt too choked to speak, like something was clogging her throat. She hadn't even considered calling him over the past few days, not with what had happened to Troy and his suspicions about Jasper Whitlaw barging into her life. She wanted him to be wrong about the man, but…

She couldn't bring herself to trust him, either, let alone believe anything he told her. While she wanted to know more about her past and the woman in that photograph with her, she had a feeling Whitlaw might not tell her the truth. Besides, learning more about her genetics didn't seem to matter much right now when she wasn't sure she and Troy had a future together, much less a future family.

"Why haven't you called me, little girl?" he asked. "Don't you care where you came from? Or do you think you're too good for me because you're a Colton now?"

She cleared her throat of the fear and dread that had caused it to clog. That fear wasn't for herself now. "What do you know about the Coltons?" she asked.

Whitlaw smirked. "More than you probably think I know. Probably more than a lot of people in this town know about them."

About the tragedy that had brought them here to start a new life in Shelby? Was that what he was alluding to? And how would he know about that?

She jumped up from her desk, sending her chair rolling across the polished concrete floor. "Stay away from them," she said.

The older man snorted. "Why? Don't you want them to know that your daddy's come back for you?"

"I'm not a little girl anymore," she said.

His beady gaze flicked over her in a way that a father should never look at his daughter. "You look so damn much like her..."

"Where is she?" she asked, wondering about her biological mother.

"If you'd called me, I might have told you," he said. "But I've been sitting around this crappy town waiting for my phone to ring, and I'm not feeling quite so talkative anymore."

"What do you want?" she asked. She was pretty sure that Troy was right now. Her father, or whoever this man was, hadn't reached out to her because he cared about her. He didn't even know her.

"Well..." He smirked again. "I could use some money. I've been sleeping in my truck because I can't afford a place around here."

"You were the one who broke into my cabin," she said. "And stole that food."

He snorted. "I shouldn't have to *break* into anything. You should be begging me to stay with you. I'm the only real family you have left, little girl."

She gasped with shock, even though she had always suspected that her biological mother wasn't alive. Surely she would have sought Lakin out sooner if she had been.

She leaned closer to him and lowered her voice even though no one else was around to overhear them. "The Coltons are my real family," she said. They had been there for her after her biological family abandoned her.

But what if her mother hadn't abandoned her?

"Well, if you don't want me bothering your *real family* for money, you better help me out." Whitlaw held his tobacco-stained hand across her desk, palm up.

Her face flushed with embarrassment and anger. Embarrassment that Troy was right and that she could potentially be related to this mercenary man. And anger that he was threatening the Coltons, the people who'd loved and raised her like their own.

"You don't want to help out your own father?" Whitlaw asked.

She nearly shuddered at the thought of this man being related to her. But she didn't want him bothering her mom and dad, so she opened the bottom drawer of the big desk and reached inside her purse for her wallet. She didn't carry much cash, so she only had a couple of twenties to hand over to him.

He stared down at the two bills lying in his palm as if waiting for her to produce more. "That's all you got?"

"Yes, it is," she said.

"This isn't nearly enough."

"For what?" she asked.

"For a room. Hell, even for much of a meal," he said. "And I'm really hungry right now."

"It's all I have," she said. And unfortunately, until her business loan was approved, she didn't have much money in the bank, either.

He snorted again. "Like you keep telling me, you're a Colton now, little girl. I don't believe you can't get your hands on more than this." He wadded up the bills in his fist.

She found herself instinctively stepping back from the desk. Maybe he wouldn't have hit her, but she had the uneasy feeling again that he knew more about the Coltons than maybe even some of the Shelby townspeople knew. Like he knew how much money they'd had before Will and Ryan had moved here and started their adventure business. Like he knew about the real estate business in California…

But how? Who the hell was he really?

Before she could ask, the office's front door opened. Whoever had taken the fishing tour, Spence or Parker, had probably returned, maybe with some clients.

But she couldn't see around Whitlaw. He leaned closer and whispered, "You better get more because I'll be back for it." Then he turned and walked away from her, right past Troy and Spence who'd just stepped inside the office.

Lakin held her breath until the door closed behind him, then released it in a ragged sigh of relief that he was gone.

For now.

She believed him, though. He would be back because he definitely wanted more than forty dollars from her. But she wasn't sure that money was really all he wanted.

Troy glanced at the door as it closed behind the older man, then he turned back toward Lakin. She looked as shaken as she'd been the day she came home from Roasters after meeting a man claiming he was her father.

"Is that him?" Troy asked, his heart thumping with anger that the man had upset her again.

"Who?" Spence asked curiously. "Who was that? A client?"

Lakin shook her head. "Nobody. That was nobody." She stared hard at Troy as if silently willing him to shut up. Then she turned toward her cousin. "Spence, I left some messages on your desk."

Spence glanced between her and Troy. "Trying to get rid of me? Okay." He headed toward his office, leaving them alone.

The old man must have been watching her and waiting for another chance to catch her alone. Troy cursed himself that Lakin had been alone. But he'd had another physical therapy session. And he'd thought her brother and cousin would be here with her.

Troy turned around and headed toward the door, but before he reached it, Lakin caught up with him.

She stepped in front of him. "Let him go."

He shook his head. "We need to find out who the hell he really is and what he wants." And if he was the one who'd been following her and who ran Troy off the road.

But Lakin remained planted in front of the door. "I don't want you going after him," she said.

Troy wondered if she was trying to protect that man or him. "What happened, Lakin? Why was he here?"

Her face flushed.

"Money," he surmised.

She closed her eyes.

Troy touched her face, running his fingertips along her jaw. "I'm sorry."

She opened her eyes, and tears glistened in them. "You were right."

"I wish I was wrong." About that, and about not committing to her. But he'd spent the past few days in physical therapy and was no closer to getting back to work on the oil rigs. If he even had a job to go back to…

And Jasper Whitlaw, or whoever he really was, wasn't the only one who needed money. Lakin needed it, too; her business loan hadn't come through yet. The last thing she needed was someone else wanting something from her instead of giving it. While Troy couldn't help her financially, he could keep her safe.

"We need to call the police," he said.

"Over a relative asking me for money?"

"You don't even know if he's a relative," he reminded her. "Someone needs to check him out." Troy would do that, or at least talk to the man, if she'd get out of his way. But Whitlaw was probably long gone by now. He would be back, though; Troy had no doubt about that.

"I'll call Eli," she said.

"You were supposed to call him days ago," he reminded her.

"I…" Clearly, she dreaded making the call. Maybe she'd hoped that Whitlaw would go away, that he'd abandon her again like when she was three.

But the man wasn't going anywhere until he got what he wanted. Money… Or more?

"Call Eli now," Troy told her. Even though he wished he could help her with Whitlaw, he didn't have the resources that Eli had. All that really mattered was that someone investigated the guy. "Call him now." He stepped back and gestured for her to return to her desk.

But when she did, she didn't reach for her phone. She glanced instead toward the back office where Spence had gone. "I will call him. I promise I will," she said, "but after I leave work." Evidently, she didn't want Parker and Spence to overhear her conversation with the ABI lieutenant.

But Troy believed the more people who knew about Whitlaw, the more they could keep an eye out for the opportunist or whatever else he might be. "Lakin, the man could be dangerous," he warned, especially if he was the person who ran Troy off the road.

"He's not going to get any more money out of me if he hurts me," she pointed out. "He's not going to hurt me."

That was really Troy's biggest concern: her safety. But he also hated seeing her as upset as this man made her.

"Just promise me you'll call Eli as soon as possible," Troy urged.

"I will, once I'm done working..." She peered around him as the outside door opened again.

Troy tensed. Had the man returned already?

But the guy who walked into the office was younger than Whitlaw. He wore the name brand adventure gear of someone with a lot of disposable income. The watch on his wrist advertised his wealth as well.

"Mr. Seller," Lakin greeted the man.

"Eric, please, Lakin, do I have to beg you to use my name?" he asked and chuckled. Then he looked at Troy standing over her desk and grinned. "So the boyfriend is home from the oil rigs." He thrust out his hand toward Troy. "Good to finally meet you."

Troy shook the man's hand but just nodded.

"You should be down on your knees," Seller said, "begging this woman to become your wife."

Troy sucked in a breath at the unsolicited advice.

"If you don't, I'm afraid you're going to lose her to someone else," Seller warned him.

"I trust Lakin," Troy said. And he did. He'd never had any reason to doubt her love or her loyalty to him.

Unfortunately she no longer believed the same of him. He hadn't called her when he was hurt, and now she didn't think he loved and needed her as much as he did. The problem was that he didn't want to need her too much. He didn't want to be like Jasper Whitlaw, a drain on her emotionally and physically.

Seller chuckled. "Even trustworthy people get sick of waiting around."

"I don't think this is really any of your business," Troy said, bristling with anger.

Lakin stood up. "Please, Troy, just leave. I need to help Mr. Seller."

Seller gave him that infuriating, condescending grin again. Troy's hand tightened into a fist that he was tempted to swing at the smug, rich guy.

"Hey, Troy," Spence said, stepping out of his office. "Let's go for that beer you promised me."

"I didn't—"

Spence wound his arm around his shoulders and started pushing him toward the outside door. "Right now."

"But—" He didn't want to leave Lakin alone with this man any more than he wanted her left alone with Jasper Whitlaw.

"Lakin's going to be a while yet, and you and I have some catching up to do," Spence said.

Troy hadn't had a chance to talk to his sister's fiancé much yet, but he'd rather put it off for another
time. Spence wasn't giving him a choice, though,
as he guided him toward the door and out into the
parking lot.

"Come on," Spence said. "Hop in my truck. You
know you're only going to piss off Lakin more if you
stick around and get into it with a client."

Troy sighed, knowing her cousin was right. He
had already pissed off Lakin when he hadn't called
her after his accident. If he didn't want her to break
up with him completely, he had to make sure that he
didn't upset her any more than he already had.

And Parker was walking up to the office now
with what looked like a couple of fishermen, so she
wouldn't be alone with Seller. And once the office
closed for the day, she would call Eli. Lakin kept
her promises.

When Troy moved around to the passenger's side
of Spence's vehicle, he noted the collection of cigarette butts on the ground in the empty spot next to it.
Somebody had either cleaned out their ashtray in the
parking lot, or they'd been standing there for a while.

Watching Lakin?

Since Hetty's brother had been back in town,
Spence had noticed the tension between Troy and
Lakin. Hetty had even mentioned it to Spence along
with her concern that her brother was going to blow
it with Lakin. Spence had managed to stop him this

time from swinging his clenched fist at a client, but he didn't know what else he could do to help ease the tension between them.

"What's going on with you and my cousin?" Spence asked once they settled onto stools at the bar.

Troy groaned, but Spence wasn't sure if it was because of Lakin or because of his back. Hetty had also filled him in on the nearly fatal accident her brother had had while working on the oil rigs.

"She's mad at me for not reaching out when I was in the hospital," Troy said.

"Hetty and your mother aren't exactly thrilled with you over that, either," Spence warned him.

Troy smiled. "I can deal with them being upset with me."

"Really?" Spence asked. "Because Hetty's got quite the temper." He'd set it off a lot before they finally realized how they really felt about each other.

"Does she get mad because you try to protect her?" Troy asked.

"Yeah," Spence said. But he wondered if they were still talking about Hetty now. He studied the younger man's face. The poor guy looked miserable and a little scared. "Is everything okay with Lakin?"

"I told you she's mad at me," Troy said.

"Yeah, I can see that, but…" Spence sensed now that something else was going on.

"We were talking about my sister," Troy said. "And of course she's going to get pissed off if you try to protect her. Hetty prides herself on being able to take care of herself."

"She does, and she can," Spence heartily agreed. "She's tough and independent and so damn beautiful…" God, he loved that woman.

Troy groaned again. "Maybe let's not talk about my sister," he said. "Not if you're going to get all mushy about her."

Spence grinned. "I'm definitely all mushy about her," he agreed. "But you and Lakin…"

Troy's shoulders slumped as if he was carrying a heavy burden. "What about me and Lakin?"

"You two have been together for so long." Spence couldn't imagine them not being together. They'd always reminded him of his aunt and uncle; Lakin's parents had met and fallen in love in high school. Like they were going to last…

But a lot of people had lost their lives lately, proving that anything could be cut short. Lives and love.

# *Chapter 11*

Once Lakin got rid of Eric Seller, she did as she'd promised Troy and called Eli. Worried that Parker might overhear their conversation, she had asked the ABI lieutenant to come talk in person.

That had to be his knock at her cabin door. Unless Troy was back.

Or Jasper Whitlaw...

She shivered and called out, "Who's there?"

"It's me, sis," Eli called back.

She released the breath she hadn't realized she'd been holding, turned the dead bolt and let him in. "Thanks for coming out."

"I would have come earlier," he said. "But I wasn't in Shelby."

"You didn't have to drop everything," she assured him. "I could have waited."

He studied her face. "No. I don't think it could. And I wanted to see you anyway."

"Check up on me, you mean," she said with a smile.

"I've been worried about you," he said.

She released a shaky breath. "You're not the only one. Troy has been bugging me to call you."

He glanced around as if looking for her boyfriend. "He's not here? I was counting on him sticking close to you after the break-in."

"He has been," she said. But was it out of concern or obligation? She wasn't as confident of his love as she'd always been. Or maybe it wasn't his love she questioned but his commitment to a future with her. "He's with Spence now." Or at least she hoped he still was and not out trying to find Jasper Whitlaw or Eric Seller.

Eli glanced around the cabin. "You shouldn't be alone at all right now," he said.

"You sound like Troy. And like Mom and Dad who've been trying to get me to stay with them," she said. She was so glad she'd resisted the temptation of going home, though, or Whitlaw might have shown up there.

"I sound like someone who loves you then," Eli said with a slight grin.

She sighed even as a smile curved her lips. "People who love me should know that I can take care of myself," she pointed out.

"You're tough, Lakin," Eli said. "But a lot of victims were."

She sucked in a breath. *Victim.* "I'm not in danger of anyone killing me," she assured him. "I'm just…"

"What?" he asked. "What's going on?"

"I don't know," she admitted. Then she pulled the photograph out of her purse and handed it to him.

Before he even looked at it, he asked, "What's this?" Then he studied the snapshot, and his jaw clenched. "This is you...in the picture..."

"The little girl," she clarified, just in case he thought she was the woman who had to be her biological mother.

"Where did you get this?" he asked. "Did Mom and Dad have it?" Then he flipped it over, probably looking for a date like Troy had. "Jasper Whitlaw. Who is this?"

"The man in the picture," she said. "He claims he's my father."

"He can claim whatever the hell he wants," Eli said. "But he needs to prove he actually has a biological relationship to you. And even if he does, he's not your *dad*."

"No, he's not," she agreed. "That's why I haven't said anything to Mom and Dad about this, so please don't..."

"Lakin." Eli's blue eyes studied her face with the intensity he'd given the photograph moments ago. "When did this guy give you the picture? Before the break-in?"

"The morning after it," she admitted.

"I don't like this," he said. "Has he bothered you again?"

She didn't deny that he had. There was no point; she was still trembling a bit from the interaction earlier. "Today," she said. "He showed up at the office."

"What does he want from you?" he asked.

"Money," she admitted with a pang of regret that Troy had been right about him.

Eli cursed. "We really should tell everyone else about this, warn them to be on the lookout."

She shook her head. "Mom and Dad are already on edge because of this serial killer. I don't want to needlessly put them through anything else. I gave Whitlaw forty bucks, so he knows I don't have much money. Maybe he'll just leave town now."

"He wants more than forty bucks, Lakin," Eli said. "He's going to be back. And I want you to keep your distance. Make sure you're never alone with him."

She nodded. "I'll be careful."

"You said Troy bugged you to call me," Eli said. "So he knows about this guy?"

She nodded again. "Yes."

"And clearly he doesn't trust him anymore than I do," Eli surmised.

She smiled. "You're both cynical and overly suspicious."

"That doesn't mean we're wrong."

She sighed. "No, it doesn't." She didn't trust Whitlaw, either. She hadn't when she first met him and she definitely didn't now after how he acted in the office. He'd barely disguised his threats to go to her family for money. "I... I'm worried," she admitted. "I don't want him bothering Mom and Dad."

"Or you," Eli said. "I'll check him out. And then I'll track him down and have a little talk with him."

She smiled. "You mean you'll run him out of town like it's the Wild West?"

"Something like that," he said with a grin.

"Before you run him out of town, can you do me a favor?" she asked.

Eli's grin slipped away. "What?"

"Can you find out what happened back then? Why I was left at the grocery store and what happened to her..." She pointed toward the photograph he held. "To my biological mother."

"He didn't tell you anything?"

She shook her head. "But he said he's the only family I have left."

"That's bullshit. You have us."

She hugged him and held on for a long moment. "I know. That's what I told him."

"And you have Troy and all of the Amos family, too," Eli reminded her.

That was what Troy had told those playground bullies all those years ago. She smiled. "But I don't want Troy fighting my battles anymore." She didn't want Eli fighting them, either, but at least he was armed. She wasn't, and neither was Troy. And she had a feeling that Troy was right about Jasper Whitlaw being dangerous. At least to her and her family.

What about Troy? Was Whitlaw the one who'd run him off the road?

Was Troy in danger, too?

"So the honeymoon is over," Hetty remarked as she joined Troy and Spence at the bar.

"Honeymoon?" Troy asked. Hetty had admitted

she'd fallen for her former nemesis, but he hadn't thought they were doing more than dating right now.

She chuckled. "Metaphorically. Instead of rushing home to me, my man is out drinking in the bars."

Spence chuckled, too, and looped his arms around her waist, pulling her in for a kiss.

Troy shook his head. "I can't believe you two are together. Not after all the trash you talked about him, Hetty."

Instead of being embarrassed or remorseful, his sister laughed.

"She stills talks trash about me," Spence said.

"No, I tell you to take out the trash," she corrected him, but from the twinkle in both their eyes, it was clear they were teasing each other.

Maybe that was all they'd ever been doing even back when they fought with each other.

"She's as bossy as ever," Spence said.

Troy groaned. "Don't I know it."

"I wouldn't have to be so bossy if you two would just do what I told you to," she said.

Spence laughed, then saluted her. "Yes, ma'am, from now on."

"Don't encourage her," Troy warned him. "She'll just get worse."

Hetty slapped his shoulder, and he flinched as his back muscles tightened. "Oh, God, I'm sorry, Troy!"

"I'm fine," he said. "I just did a lot of physical therapy today." He had been daily; he needed to get stronger.

"Is it going well?" she asked, her green eyes bright with concern.

"It's getting better," he said. He probably wouldn't hurt like he did now if he wasn't so tense from finding Lakin alone in the office with Whitlaw. And then the other guy, Seller, warning him about losing her...

"And your relationship with Lakin?" Troy probably flinched again because Hetty added, "That's too bad."

He sighed.

"She still hasn't forgiven you for not calling her when you fell?" Hetty asked. "That doesn't sound like Lakin. She loves you so much, and she's so forgiving. Unlike me and Mom. We're still pissed as hell at you." She reached out as if to smack his shoulder again but pulled her hand back before making contact.

"I understand why you're all mad about that," Troy admitted. "I would be, too."

"But you would do the same thing all over again, wouldn't you?" Hetty asked. "You wouldn't call any of us until you knew if and how you were going to recover."

His sister knew him well. He nodded. "I didn't want to upset anyone until I knew what I was dealing with. And I sure as hell don't want to be a burden to anyone."

Hetty snorted. "No, you want to be the hero, Troy. And you don't have to be. You just have to be you. That's who we all love."

"I like him a lot, but love..." Spence shrugged. "I don't know."

Hetty laughed and lightly swatted her boyfriend's

shoulder. "I know you love him, too. All of you Coltons love my brother Troy."

The Coltons had always been so warm and friendly to him. While they were that way with everyone, they'd made him feel special in that they'd taken the time to get to know him. Sometimes, growing up in a big family like his, Troy had felt lost in the shuffle. Unimportant. But the Coltons had always made him feel special; no one more so than Lakin. She'd always looked at him like he was her hero.

And he didn't want her to stop looking at him that way, or worse yet, to look at him with pity instead. "I just want to make sure that I'll be able to work again," he said. "I want to take care of Lakin, not have her take care of me."

Hetty shook her head. "Your damn pride, Troy. It's going to be your downfall. Lakin doesn't care about money or anything else but *you*."

Hetty didn't know Lakin like he did; she didn't know about Lakin's dreams, about the hotel she'd already purchased and the family she wanted to have.

Troy didn't want to hold back the woman he loved from achieving everything she wanted. He didn't want to tie her to his uncertain future. That was why he hadn't begged her to marry him like Seller had told him he should. If Troy knew he had a job and a way to help her out with the business and with the children she wanted to have, he would hit his knees and propose right now.

But he had a feeling that even if he did, Lakin might not accept. He might have already done too much damage to their relationship. He might have hurt her too much for her to trust him completely with her heart.

Once Eli reluctantly left his sister's cabin, he wasted no time running a background check on Jasper Whitlaw. To verify the man's real name, Eli had even taken fingerprints from the photograph he'd borrowed from Lakin.

She wanted it back. Hell, she hadn't wanted to part with it at all.

He could understand why. That photograph was the one link to her past and the people who might be able to answer questions about it. Like why she'd been left in that grocery store all those years ago.

Jasper Whitlaw might have those answers, but he would obviously only give them to her if she paid for them. And then it wasn't a guarantee that he would actually tell her the truth about anything.

A quick background search was enough for Eli to conclude that this man was probably not her father. So what was he? Besides a convicted criminal? The man had been in prison until recently, so maybe that was why he hadn't sought out Lakin sooner.

But why now? What did he want from her?

Money or silence?

Did Lakin know more about her past than she was willing to remember?

# Chapter 12

Lakin drove her SUV into the empty parking lot of the former Shelby Hotel, then looked around before getting out and heading toward the door to the lounge area. She was pretty sure she was still being followed. She just wasn't sure who it was now. A random stalker? Jasper Whitlaw? Troy or one of her brothers?

They were all worried about her. She was worried, too, but not so much about being watched as about her future plans. She and Troy were stuck in this kind of limbo where he wanted to protect her but not be her partner. So he slept on the couch, and she wasn't sure that she slept at all.

She lay in bed with her body aching for his. Usually when he returned from being away, they rarely left her bed. This time they had only made love once. She was going slowly out of her mind with frustration and desire for him. She wanted him so damn badly.

She wasn't at all sure that he felt the same. Maybe it was easier for him to ignore the attraction because he wasn't fully recovered from his fall.

While he went to physical therapy nearly every day, he seemed to be in more pain, not less, after his sessions. Maybe he was pushing himself too hard to heal. He probably wanted to get right back to work on the oil rigs that had killed his father and had almost killed him as well.

She wasn't sure she could keep sending him off with a smile and the hope that he would come home to her. Because he might not...

She pressed a hand over her heart at the horrific thought and the physical pain it brought her. She didn't want to lose Troy, but she felt in some ways she already had. She'd lost the Troy that for the past ten years she'd planned a future with; she'd lost the man she'd envisioned as her partner in business and life.

Tears blurred her vision, and she had to blink them away to unlock the door. Her hand trembled, and she still struggled to get the door opened. Then she realized she'd locked it.

It must have already been unlocked.

But how? She was the only one with a key, or so she'd been told. But from the condition of them, it didn't look as if the locks had been changed recently. Maybe whoever had keys from when it was still the Shelby Hotel had used them to stop in and look at the place.

She hoped that was all they'd done. She wanted to get the place up and running as quickly as possible. She had to if she was going to pay her dad back as fast as she'd promised.

He'd told her to take her time; he'd even offered her more money. But she wanted to do this on her own.

No. She wanted to do this with Troy.

But if he was here, he was probably out in his old truck watching her. Hopefully he was the only one.

A thump and then a tinkle of breaking glass startled her. It came from somewhere inside the hotel.

And she realized she was not alone. Nobody would have broken into a long abandoned hotel to find food.

So why were they here?

What did they want?

The physical therapist had turned him away today. "You're exhausted. You need to rest."

But Troy wasn't tired because of therapy; he was tired because he couldn't sleep with Lakin so close and yet so far from his reach. She hadn't just shut him out of her bedroom; it was as if she was shutting him out of her life, too.

Or maybe he'd shut himself out, just like Hetty had warned him. Being too stubborn and too proud.

He really didn't want to be Lakin's hero, like Hetty had accused him of wanting; he just didn't want to be a burden to her. He wanted her to be happy and, more important, safe.

To ensure her safety, he'd followed her from the RTA office over to the old Shelby Hotel. He waited until she'd parked and gone inside before he pulled into the parking lot. Weeds were growing through the asphalt because nobody had been using it. The building looked as abandoned as the parking lot; its windows were all boarded up. The wood siding was weathered and, in some places, rotted. The place needed a lot of work.

But of course, Lakin would see the potential in it. Just as she must have seen the potential in him all those years ago. She was always so positive and hopeful until recently. Until he'd hurt her.

His heart hurt more than his back that he'd done that. He'd let her down in more ways than one. First, he hadn't told her when he was in the hospital, and second, he didn't reply to her texts and emails about the hotel.

But Troy loved her too much to saddle her with a cripple, which he might wind up being if he got hurt again. He wanted to be an asset to her, not a liability. He just wasn't sure how he could help her except to keep her safe right now.

While she'd talked to Eli like she'd promised, Troy wasn't sure what else her oldest brother was doing to protect her. Ideally the ABI lieutenant would have run Jasper Whitlaw out of town, but Troy was pretty sure he'd seen the man skulking around town still.

Whitlaw drove an old pickup truck like Troy's, like Billy Hoover's. And Whitlaw was always somewhere in the vicinity of Lakin, like Troy was. Strangely enough, sometimes Billy Hoover was, too.

Troy didn't trust their old school bully any more than he trusted the stranger claiming to be Lakin's father. With those two never far away from her, not to mention that bored rich RTA client Eric Seller, Troy needed to stick even closer to her.

He pushed open the door to his truck and stepped out onto the cracked asphalt of the old parking lot. He waited for his back muscles to tighten from twisting himself out from under the steering wheel. But he didn't feel even a twinge of discomfort. Maybe the physical therapy was helping. Maybe he would recover enough to be the partner Lakin deserved to have.

Feeling a little lighter and more hopeful, he studied the hotel for a moment. Instead of seeing the boarded-up windows and weathered wood, he saw the potential that Lakin must have seen. The location was great, and the structure itself looked solid. The roof wasn't sagging, and the walls were straight. It might not take as much time and money and manpower as he thought to renovate it into something special.

Lakin wasn't just optimistic; she was smart. And she was gutsy as hell to have gone ahead and bought this property at an auction with no chance for inspections or way to back out of it. But because she was so smart and determined, he knew that she would work hard and make it a success.

He felt a yearning to be part of it, part of her dream, of her future with this business and with a family. With a little girl who looked like that little girl in the photograph Whitlaw had given Lakin.

He headed toward the front door, eager to see inside the building.

When he put his hand on the knob, he heard Lakin's scream.

Chilled, he tried the knob. It didn't move.

She'd locked herself inside with whatever danger she faced.

"I just want to shake him," Hetty said, frustration overwhelming her.

Her mother chuckled. "You used to say that all the time about Spence Colton."

Now Hetty wanted to do more than shake Spence Colton. She smiled but then remembered why she was frustrated and frowned. "I'm talking about my idiot brother."

Her mother sighed. "He's more stubborn than your father."

"He's trying to be Dad," Hetty said. "Sacrificing everything to take care of everyone else. He's going to lose Lakin if he doesn't realize he doesn't have to be her hero. He just has to be her partner." Like she and Spence were partners. Equals. Both independent and strong separately but even stronger together. They'd had to be, or they wouldn't have survived when a professional assassin had tried to kill them.

"Why would he feel like he has to be her hero?" Mom asked. "Is something going on with Lakin?"

Hetty tensed. Was there something going on with Lakin? Was there a reason her brother felt as if he had to protect the woman he loved? From what? How could Lakin, who didn't have an enemy in the world, be in danger?

Then Hetty remembered how she and Spence had just been in the wrong place at the wrong time and nearly lost their lives because of it. And those women…

The poor women who'd become victims of a serial killer. Had they even realized they were in danger before it was too late? Was that who Troy thought he needed to protect Lakin from? A serial killer?

Or was there another threat against her?

If there was, Hetty had no doubt that Troy would do whatever he could to protect her from it, like putting himself in danger to save her.

# Chapter 13

Lakin's throat burned from the scream. She'd uttered it as much to scare off whoever was in the hotel with her as to call for help. She just wasn't sure if anyone was close enough to hear her.

The front door behind her burst open with such force it slammed against the wall. Troy ran inside and put his hands on her shoulders.

"What is it?" he asked. "What's wrong?"

"Someone's in here," she whispered.

He let go of her and rushed off, intent on rescuing her as usual. Just like he'd chased the intruder from her cabin into the woods that first day back in Shelby.

But he wasn't limping today.

Lakin struggled to keep up with him as he ran through the lounge and down a wide hall. He opened each door off the hallway. Finally he stopped outside one, and Lakin caught up with him, peering over his shoulder into the room, she saw shattered glass sparkle in the sunlight pouring through an open window.

"Someone took the boards off from the outside," she said, keeping her voice low.

"They didn't get inside," he said, pointing to a small hole in the glass. Someone had hit it with some kind of tool, probably whatever they'd used to pry off the boards. But they hadn't gotten through the window.

Maybe her scream had scared them off. She released a shaky breath of relief.

Troy spun away from the window as if to head outside.

She grasped his arm. "Stop." She didn't want him getting hurt because of whatever was going on with her. "I'll call the police."

"Whoever it is will be gone by the time Officer Reynolds gets here."

"Whoever it was is probably already gone," she pointed out.

Troy tugged his arm from her grasp and hurried from the room, as if trying to prove her wrong. Or catch the would-be intruder.

She hoped she was right and that the person was long gone. Or Troy could be running into danger.

Troy was too late to catch this intruder, just as he'd been too damn late at her cabin. The only thing left behind, besides the splintered boards pried from the window, was a cigarette butt.

He stared down at it and at the boot prints left next to it. The prints were similar to the ones he'd found in the woods when her cabin had been broken into. "It has to be Whitlaw," he said.

"Why?" Lakin asked. "What does he have to gain by breaking into places I own?" She gestured at the back of the building where the window had been broken. The wood was even more weathered than on the front. "There's nothing to steal in there. Or in my cabin."

"Maybe he's just trying to scare you," Troy said. "So that you'll give him what he wants."

"Money." She snorted. "Joke's on him. I'm broke after buying this place."

Troy flinched, not with pain but with regret. He had some money saved up that he could give her, but he wasn't sure how long he would be without work. He'd already lost weeks of wages. In trying to get some compensation for that, he was probably going to lose his job, too. While he didn't have many expenses of his own, he also didn't want to have to borrow money from anyone.

"I know that was my choice," she said. "But I didn't want to lose this place. I can see it so clearly, how amazing it can be." She smiled as she stared at the building. "I think I'll call it Suite Home."

"Sweet?"

"S-u-i-t-e," she spelled out. "Each room will be a suite with a little kitchenette and a spa-like bathroom. There will also be space for a work area and of course a very nice bed."

He could see it, too. "It's going to take money to make all those changes."

Her smile slipped away.

And he could have cursed himself for dimming her excitement.

"It's all about money with you, Troy." She glanced down at the cigarette butt.

"It's all about money for a lot of people," he said.

"Well, Whitlaw isn't going to get any more out of me," she said.

"You paid him?" he asked with alarm. "When? Have you seen him again?" He should have stuck closer to her.

"I haven't seen him since that day you found him in the office with me. That was when I gave him forty bucks," she said. "That was all I had in my wallet at the time."

"It's not all the money that the Coltons have," he pointed out.

Her father had helped her buy the hotel at auction; he would help her pay off that creep, too. But giving Whitlaw any money probably wouldn't get rid of him. It would just make him greedy for more.

"I'm not asking my dad for any more money," she said. "The bank is waiting on the professional appraisal of the hotel, and then I should be approved for my business loan." But she looked more nervous than confident. "I'm going to make this place a success."

He nodded. "I know you will, Lakin."

"Do it with me," she implored him. "Be my partner."

His chest ached with the urge to say yes. "I just need another year on the oil rigs, and then I'll have enough money—"

"No!" she exclaimed, her voice sharp. "You can't be serious about going back to work on them. Putting your life in danger again?"

He might not be able to go back to work there if he was fired. "I have Mitch helping me with something that could make the workplace safer from now on. All the safety harnesses will be regularly inspected and any ones with the frayed ropes like mine would be thrown out."

"How is Mitch helping you with that?" she asked.

"He filed a lawsuit against them in civil court," he admitted. But after his mother's civil suit had failed years ago, he knew not to get his hopes up again. "All I really want is the wages I lost when I was in the hospital and then a safer workplace going forward for my coworkers and for me." It was too late to help his dad, but Troy wanted to make sure nobody else lost their life like he did. Or got hurt like Troy had.

"It's not safe for you to go back there," she said. "Especially because you've sued them."

He snorted. "I may not be able to go back," he said. "My supervisor already made that clear to me."

"He threatened you?"

He shrugged. "I don't know. I think Harrison was just drunk when he called me and was acting like Billy Hoover. Mitch says they can't fire me over this."

"I hope they do," she said.

He gasped.

"You want to protect me," she said. "That's why you keep following me around, but you won't protect yourself." She shook her head. "You won't even listen to me. And I'm sure your mom and Hetty are begging you not to go back, too."

His face flushed a bit. "Well…"

"They don't want to lose you," she said.

"What about you, Lakin?" he asked. Had he already lost her.

"I don't want anything to happen to you, Troy. I don't want you to get hurt on the oil rigs or here in Shelby while you keep trying to protect me."

"Lakin, you must realize that you're in danger," he said, pointing toward the splintered boards. "Someone tried to get into the hotel just like they got into your cabin. You know that someone's following you."

"Yeah, you are," she said, her lips curving into a slight smile.

"I'm not the only one."

She shivered. "Have you gotten a good look at who it is?"

"Just that old truck that drove me off the road that day," he said. "But there are a lot of old trucks in Shelby."

"You could have died that day, Troy," she said. "You have to stop putting yourself in danger. Eli knows what's going on. He'll take care of it."

"Eli has a lot on his plate right now," Troy pointed out. "And he's not even around Shelby very often. He can't protect you."

Troy wasn't sure how well he could, either. He was never quite fast enough to catch whoever was after her. And that was the only way to make sure that she was safe—to catch and stop whoever was after her.

The boyfriend was a pain in the ass. He was always around, always in the way.

Maybe it was time to get a gun.

That might be the most effective way to get rid of Troy Amos.

# *Chapter 14*

Bobby Reynolds came by the hotel to check out the attempted break-in, but he wasn't too concerned. "Teenagers break into this place a lot," he said. "Looking for a place to hang out."

Lakin wished she could believe that, but it all felt too coincidental that it happened so recently after her cabin had been broken into. And why would teenagers be breaking into abandoned buildings during the daytime when they should be in school? Of course she'd been a good student who didn't skip classes, so maybe she was being naive about teenagers. Or paranoid about the break-ins. But she didn't argue with the officer.

Troy, on the other hand, wanted Bobby to track down Jasper Whitlaw and check his alibi.

Bobby warned him against making accusations with no proof. He also refused to have the cigarette butt tested for DNA since a broken window wasn't a high priority case. "Leave the policing to the police," he cautioned.

Lakin definitely didn't argue with that. Neither did

Troy, though she didn't expect him to stop trying to protect her. Fortunately he also helped her secure the hotel again so no damage should come to the place.

Despite Bobby claiming teenagers had broken into the building before, she and Troy didn't find much damage inside. The roof, while old, hadn't even leaked. It really wouldn't take much for her to fix it up and get it going. She could renovate a couple of rooms and the lounge and start on a small scale, if she couldn't secure that loan.

She was going to make it a success. Even Troy believed that. If only he would help her...

But she didn't want to beg him to build a future with her. If after ten years he couldn't commit, then, she told herself, she didn't want him.

Only she did.

Once they were back in her cabin, she found herself lingering in the living room with him instead of going into her bedroom and locking the door. As frustrated as she was with his stubborn determination to return to work on the oil rigs, she was also frustrated from denying herself the passion that always burned between them.

If he left again, she didn't want to regret not being with him. Even if it might be their last time.

"Thank you for helping me board up that window again," she said.

He nodded. "I'm sorry that's all I can do to help you at the hotel."

"That's not all you can do," she said. "It's all you're willing to do."

"Lakin, it's not that I'm not willing," he said. "I just don't know what the future holds for me, not after the accident."

"Nobody knows what the future holds, Troy," she pointed out. "We just have to have faith that everything will work out for the best."

"But it doesn't all work out for the best," he said. "My dad died. Your aunt and grandparents were murdered. Bad things happen all the time, and we don't know when or where or how they're going to happen."

She shivered at the reminder. "You're right." And because of that, she was even more determined to take what was right in front of her, while *he* was still here. She'd already nearly lost him when he fell off that rig and then the side of the mountain. She didn't want to lose him because of an accident. Or something that maybe wasn't an accident.

"I'm sorry," he said again.

"Me, too," she said. She reached out then, sliding her arms around his broad shoulders. "I'm sorry I've been locking you out."

"I understand why you're mad at me," he said.

"I don't even think I'm mad anymore..." She wasn't sure what she was now. Maybe resigned. The next time he left, he wouldn't be coming back to her even if he returned to Shelby in one piece. She wasn't going to wait around for him any longer.

"You've forgiven me?" he asked, his green eyes brightening.

She didn't want to dash his hopes like he'd dashed hers. Instead of replying, she kissed him, sliding her lips seductively back and forth across his mouth.

He clasped a hand in her hair, holding her head to his, and kissed her back. Deeply. Passionately.

Her pulse raced as heat flushed her entire body. She wanted him so damn badly. Despite all the years they'd been together the passion between them had never cooled. It burned as hot as ever, maybe even hotter now than before. Because of the danger, because of knowing how close she'd come to losing him, Lakin wanted him more than she ever had.

As she pressed her mouth hungrily to his, she tugged him back toward her bedroom. This time she wasn't locking him out; she might just lock him inside with her, to keep the rest of the world out.

He lifted his mouth from hers, panting for breath, and asked, "Are you sure, Lakin?"

She nodded. She was sure that she wanted to make love with him, but that was all she was sure of at the moment. She wasn't sure that they had a future. But she didn't want him going back to the oil rigs without being with him again, even if it was the last time.

Once in the bedroom, he kicked the door shut. And then he dragged off his clothes. He was so muscular. His biceps bulged, his ab muscles rippled, and his chest thumped, his heart beating as fast as hers.

Needing to press her skin against his, she undressed quickly, too, until she was as naked as he was. His erection pulsated, as if begging for her attention.

But before she could reach for him, he was swinging her up in his arms.

"Troy!" she exclaimed, worried that he was going to hurt himself.

He grimaced as he carried her the short couple of steps to the bed. When he laid her on it, he followed her down. She wasn't sure if it was because he wanted to be close to her or if it was because he was hurt.

"You shouldn't be overdoing it," she said. "Are you all right?"

"Frustrated," he said. "It's been killing me to lie out there on the couch, aching for you."

She didn't want him aching *because* of her, though. She wasn't petite. She was five nine with an athletic build. But Troy had always picked her up like she was light. Until today.

"Are you really all right?" she persisted.

"I will be," he said. "Once I'm inside you, once we're as close as we used to be."

Physically they could be that close again, but she wasn't sure about emotionally. But then he was touching her, sliding his hands and mouth all over her, and she couldn't think at all. She could only feel the passion burning inside her, making her tremble.

She touched him, too, running her hands and mouth over him. But before she could slide her lips around his erection, he pulled back.

"I'll go too fast," he said. "I want to take my time."

Maybe he knew, too, that this might be their last time. Their last chance to be this close. Maybe that was why he gave her so much pleasure, moving between her legs to make love to her with his mouth and his wicked tongue.

She squirmed against the blankets as he drove her wild with desire. The tension was so tight inside her, and then he moved his hands to her breasts, stroking them. She cried out as she came.

Then he was inside her, thrusting slowly, building the tension inside her again. But he knew how and where to touch her to release that tension. And she came again, screaming his name.

Then his body tensed and shuddered and he cried out her name.

And, "I love you."

She loved him, too, but she couldn't say those words right now, not when their future was so uncertain. And it wasn't just Troy going back to the oil rigs that could end their relationship but whoever was following her around and breaking into her cabin and the hotel. That person could end their relationship and maybe their lives.

She didn't say it back.

For the first time since they had exchanged *I love yous* as teenagers, Lakin didn't say it back to him. Even though they'd made love and both stayed in her bed afterward, Troy felt like he was still shut out. Not out of her bedroom but maybe out of her life and her heart.

Long after Lakin had fallen asleep, he lay awake, worrying that his sister was probably right. He was going to lose Lakin if he didn't make a commitment to her and their future.

Maybe losing her would be the best thing for her. She could have a better life with someone like that rich customer who'd also warned him about losing Lakin. Was that because he wanted her for himself?

And what about Whitlaw? What did he want from her? Just money or something more?

Eventually Troy must have fallen asleep because he awoke to sunlight slanting through the blinds to shine in his eyes. He blinked and squinted, trying to focus. But he didn't need to see anything to know that Lakin was gone. The bed was cold beside him.

Maybe she'd already left for work, or maybe she'd gone to Roasters. He didn't want her going there alone. That was where Jasper Whitlaw had first accosted her.

She'd given the photograph to Eli. But what had her big brother found out about Whitlaw? Was the older man even in town still?

Troy needed to make sure Lakin was safe. He dressed in a hurry and headed off to the coffee shop. But when he pulled into the lot, her SUV wasn't there.

Maybe he'd just missed her. But what about Jasper Whitlaw? Had he been hanging around?

Troy was sick of waiting for this guy to show up

and harass her again. He wanted to find the man and make him leave town. So he parked his truck and rushed into the café.

"Hey, are you here to pick up Lakin's order?" the barista asked him.

"Did she place an order?" he asked. Maybe she was on her way.

"No, but she usually comes in every morning, and I haven't seen her for a few days."

Because Lakin didn't want to run into the man who claimed he was her father.

"There was an older guy here the last day she was in," Troy said. "He gave her a photograph. Did you see him that day? Have you seen him around town?"

The barista's eyes widened and then narrowed. "Older guy, looks kind of homeless? I have seen him hanging around here, but that was more before he talked to Lakin. I haven't seen him often after that day he gave her something. Then she drove off with her coffee mugs on the roof of her vehicle. I picked them up and washed them for her."

"That was very sweet of you," he said.

"Lakin is sweet," the young woman said. "One of my favorite customers."

People were naturally drawn to Lakin's kindness and her beauty. He was lucky that he hadn't already lost her to someone who could give her more time and attention. Fortunately for him Lakin was as loyal and loving as she was beautiful.

Troy leaned closer to the counter. "Will you let

me know if you see that guy around here again? Or anywhere?" he asked. "I really want to talk to him."

"No." The deep voice that answered wasn't the barista's.

Troy turned around to find Lakin's oldest brother, Eli, standing behind him. His arms were crossed over his chest, and he didn't look happy.

But Troy wasn't particularly happy with him, either. Lakin had reached out to him for help, but things were still happening, like that broken window at the hotel.

Officer Reynolds might believe it was teenagers, but Troy didn't. Lakin was in danger, and Troy felt like he was the only one doing anything to protect her. He was afraid it still wasn't enough…

Eli was apparently at Roasters for the same reason that his sister's boyfriend was, and it wasn't for the coffee although it did smell damn good in the café.

"No," he repeated. "If she sees Jasper Whitlaw around again, she's going to call me." He passed the barista a card as she handed a coffee over the counter for him. He laid down some bills and turned toward Troy again. "Do you want anything?"

Troy stepped away from the counter. "Not coffee. I want answers."

Eli sighed. "Don't we all?" He had so many questions and not just about Whitlaw.

"So you haven't found out anything more about that man who accosted Lakin?" Troy asked.

Eli had, but he intended to tell Lakin first and definitely not in a public place. "I know he's dangerous," he said. "And that you shouldn't be looking to confront him."

Troy sucked in a breath, looking like Eli had punched him. "So Lakin really is in danger."

"I don't know that he would hurt her," Eli said. "He won't be able to get money out of her if he does." Though he wasn't certain that was all Whitlaw wanted from her or why he'd turned up in Shelby when he had. "But I don't think he would hesitate to hurt you if you get in his way," Eli warned the younger man. He'd always liked Troy Amos; the guy was a hard worker who clearly worshipped Lakin. If something happened to him, Lakin probably wouldn't get over it.

"I don't care what he does to me," Troy said. "I just want to make sure he doesn't hurt Lakin."

Eli figured it was already too late for that. Whitlaw's sudden appearance with the photograph had stirred up a lot of emotions for Lakin and a lot of questions about her past. Eli understood that only too well; the Fiancée Killer was stirring up a lot of memories and nightmares for him and undoubtedly for the rest of his family, too.

The last thing any of them needed was someone trying to hurt another one of their family.

"I'm on it," Eli promised him. "I'm looking for the guy, and when I find him, I'll make sure that he knows he's not getting anything out of Lakin."

"You might want to check out a couple of other guys that seem to keep turning up around her," Troy remarked.

Eli felt a smile twitch his lips. "Lakin is beautiful. I'm sure there are a lot of guys who keep turning up."

Troy looked again as if Eli had struck him.

"Didn't it occur to you that other men might find her attractive?"

"Of course," Troy said. "I'm not talking about that kind of attention. I'm talking about her old school bully, Billy Hoover, showing up here and other places unexpectedly. And then there's some RTA client, Something Seller, that seems a little too interested in her."

Eli tensed. The thought that the serial killer could be targeting someone in his family was keeping him awake nights. Why else were the murders so similar to his aunt's death? But who in Shelby really knew about his aunt Caroline and his family's reasons for moving here from California all those years ago?

"I'll check into them, too," Eli assured him. "But you need to stay out of this."

Troy shook his head. "Not until I know she's safe."

Troy Amos obviously loved Lakin a lot, so much so that he was more concerned about her life than his. But if he really knew Lakin well, he would know that she wouldn't want him getting hurt because of her.

And Eli had a feeling that, as determined as Troy was to protect her, he probably was going to wind up getting hurt or worse.

# *Chapter 15*

Leaving Troy lying alone in her bed had been hard. After last night, after being that close to him again, Lakin wanted to stay curled up in his arms with her head on his chest. But she knew that eventually they would have to talk, and every time they spoke lately, she was disappointed that Troy was so uncertain about their future.

He should know that it didn't matter to her if he wasn't able to work again; she loved him for who he was, not for the money he might make someday. Maybe he knew how she felt, but he was just too proud to accept her unconditional love if he couldn't give her what he wanted to in return.

She blinked hard to focus on her computer screen, and a sigh slipped out along with all her frustration. She was too much in limbo right now, waiting to find out if Troy would recover fully, waiting for her business loan, waiting to find out if Jasper Whitlaw was really her biological father so she could get some answers about her past.

She cared the least about Whitlaw. He'd waited

more than twenty years before finding her, so he didn't care about her. She couldn't trust whatever he told her. And the past didn't matter as much as her present and her future.

If she and Troy even had one…

"You look very stressed for someone so young," a voice remarked.

Startled that she wasn't alone, Lakin jumped, making her chair creak. A hand touched her shoulder, maybe just to steady her, but she jumped up from her chair at the unwelcome contact and so that Eric Seller wasn't standing over her anymore like he had been. "Are you okay?" he asked.

She shook her head. "I didn't hear you come into the office."

"You need one of those bells that ding when the door opens," he suggested.

Usually people didn't slip in so silently, so it had never been an issue before. Although Jasper Whitlaw had the other day.

"Do you need something?" she asked. She hadn't even realized that he'd signed up for another tour. But then she'd been distracted lately and not really doing her job as well as she should. She needed to talk to Parker and give her notice.

"I was just thinking about you, Lakin, and wanted to make sure that you're okay," he said.

Instead of reassuring her, his words made her more uneasy than she usually was around him. "I'm fine," she said. "No need to worry about me." And definitely no reason to make a special trip to Shelby.

"I've seen all the news about some serial killer targeting single women in this area," he said. "So naturally I thought of you."

"I'm not single," she said.

"You're not married," he said. "Or even engaged. You could be a potential target."

She shivered. "With some of the victims not even identified yet, nobody knows if they were single or not. So are you just trying to scare me?" she asked. And it was working since she wondered how he knew something that hadn't been disclosed in the press.

His eyes widened as if in surprise. "Oh, I guess I just assumed that they were all single. And I think, that with you looking similar to previous victims and being alone so often, you need to be extra careful."

"I am," she assured him or maybe she was warning him.

He glanced around the office. "Really? You're all alone here. Even that boyfriend of yours isn't hanging around..." He took a step closer, as if he'd been waiting for the opportunity to get her alone.

She opened her mouth and considered releasing a scream but instead she shouted, "I'm not alone!" And hoped like hell she was telling the truth because she wasn't sure what Seller was trying to do.

"Lakin!" Parker exclaimed, appearing suddenly in the doorway of his office. "What's going on?" He looked from her to Seller. "Is there a problem?"

Seller shook his head and stepped back from her desk. "No problem at all. I'm just very concerned about your sister."

"Why?" Parker asked with his usual bluntness.

"Just seems like Shelby is a dangerous place for a single woman," Seller said.

Parker snorted. "Lakin isn't single. She's been with Troy Amos for most of their lives, and he will make damn certain nothing happens to her."

"Really?" Seller asked. "I understand that he isn't usually around that much."

Lakin nearly screamed now—with irritation, not fear. "I can take care of myself," she assured them both.

"But there's a serial killer on the loose," Seller said. "His other victims probably thought the same thing you do, that they could take care of themselves."

Other victims. Was he saying that she was going to be next?

"Are you trying to scare her?" Parker asked. "And what are you doing here? You don't have a reservation, and we're completely booked."

Which was a lie. There had been a few cancellations, probably because of the serial killer scaring away some of their clients.

Seller held up his hands. "I'm sorry. I should have called ahead to make sure there was availability. I just had some downtime and came up for a quick fishing trip."

"You must have a lot of downtime," Parker re-marked. "You're here a lot."

Had any of Seller's visits coincided with when those women disappeared? Lakin wanted to ask, but she didn't want to accuse one of their most fre-quent guests of being a serial killer. Although she suspected that her brother shared her suspicions. Parker moved even closer to them.

"I really enjoy my time in Shelby," Seller said. "I like to visit as often as I can. Let me know if you have a cancellation today. I'll take myself to that coffee shop in town for now. I can see that I've made you both uneasy. That was never my intention."

Lakin wasn't so sure about that.

Apparently neither was Parker. He didn't say any-thing else to Seller, just watched him until he left the building. Then he turned toward her. "Are you okay? I can refuse his business from now on and keep him away from you."

"I love you for offering to do that," she said. "But he's a great client."

"Not if he's creeping on you," Parker said. "I don't like how he was talking to you."

"Neither do I," she admitted. "But I'm just going to ignore him from now on."

"I don't think that's a good idea, either," Parker said. "We should talk to Eli about him. The com-ments he made about those victims..." He shuddered.

She nodded. "I agree that Eli should check him out." She didn't want anyone getting hurt because she had been too naive to believe someone she knew could be dangerous. She had a feeling that Seller wasn't the only person she knew who could be, though.

Parker nodded. "I'll give our big brother a call—"

"Wait," she said.

"You changed your mind? You think Seller is okay?"

"No. I just want to talk to you for a minute," she said. "I've been meaning to do it..." since she'd bought the hotel.

"What's going on, Lakin?" Parker asked with concern.

"I've been wanting to start my own business for a while now," she said.

"This is your business, too," Parker said, gesturing with open arms. "This is our family business."

"This is your business now," she said. "Since Dad and Uncle Ryan retired, you've taken over. You're the one who's made it more successful than it's ever been."

He shook his head. "No. That's been all of us working hard together."

She smiled. "I love working here, but I want to do what you've done. I want to take something and put all my energy into rebuilding it into what I want."

"Like what?" he asked.

"Like the Shelby Hotel."

"I thought that recently sold at auction," he replied.

"It did," she said, "to me."

"That's great, Lakin!" Parker hugged her, then pulled back. "But damn, that place needs a lot of work."

She nodded. "I know. That's why I'm going to need to devote all my time and energy to it."

"You're leaving?"

Tears stung her eyes at the thought of no longer working with her brother in the family business, but she nodded. "Yes, but I'll keep working here until you find my replacement."

"Nobody will ever be able to replace you," Parker said and hugged her again. "What about Troy? Will he be helping you?"

More tears rushed to her eyes, but she blinked them away, too. "I don't know."

"He was hurt on that damn oil rig," Parker said. "He's not going to go back, is he?"

"I hope not," she said. "But I think he will if he can."

"And leave you again? Leave you to do all the work at the hotel alone?"

"You know I won't be alone," she said.

Parker chuckled. "No, Dad is always looking for a new hobby."

"He helped me buy it," she admitted. "I'm going to pay him back, though, as soon as my business loan gets approved."

"I'm glad he has something else to think about," Parker said.

"Other than RTA?"

"Other than the Fiancée Killer."

She shuddered at the mention of the serial killer.

"You really need to be careful," Parker said. "The way Seller was talking…"

"I know," she agreed. "And I will be." But like Seller had pointed out, the serial killer's victims probably all thought they were being careful, too.

Troy was beyond pissed that Eli wouldn't tell him why he knew Jasper Whitlaw was dangerous. After his frustrating conversation with the ABI lieutenant, he left Roasters and headed straight to the RTA office…and walked into another tense conversation between Lakin and Parker.

They both assured him that everything was fine, but he had his suspicions, especially when they confirmed he had seen that Seller guy leaving. Troy was glad he'd given the man's name to Eli.

The office got busy after that, and neither Lakin nor Parker had time to talk. Neither did Hetty when she rushed in for a minute before leaving for a flight. All she said was, "Mom and I have been talking about you."

"That's nothing new," he replied with a chuckle.

"Do us all a favor," she said with a glance at Lakin who was on a call and hopefully not listening. "Stay here in Shelby. No more oil rigs. No more danger."

Even if he promised no more oil rigs, he couldn't promise no more danger. Nobody could. But Hetty rushed off again before he could point that out to her. Hell, not too long ago she'd been shot. She knew as did everyone who watched the news that Shelby wasn't safe at all anymore.

Once Lakin had a free moment, Troy told her about his conversation with Eli.

She nodded, unsurprised. "He texted me earlier. He's going to come by later this afternoon and fill me in," she said.

"Good."

"That means that you don't have to babysit me," she said. "You must be bored sitting around all day watching me."

"Never," he said. And it was true. He missed her so much when he was gone that he could never see enough of her to make up for it. Maybe Hetty was right; maybe it was time that he gave up working on the oil rigs. But what could he do in Shelby that would make enough money to help his family and Lakin with her business?

"Seriously, Troy, you don't need to be here," Lakin said. "There are a lot of people coming and going, and Eli will be here soon."

"Sounds like she's trying to get rid of you," Parker remarked when he stepped out of his office.

"That goes for you, too," she said. "You've been hovering."

"After that conversation this morning, I don't think you should be alone."

"Conversation?" Troy repeated. "What conversation? With Seller? What happened?"

Lakin sighed. "I don't want to rehash all this. And Eli is on his way. You can both take off. Go get a beer. Something."

It was obvious she didn't want him or Parker around when she talked to the ABI lieutenant. Or maybe she didn't want Troy around at all anymore. Maybe last night had been a goodbye. A last time...

The thought jabbed his heart with a sudden pain.

"You look like you could use a beer," Parker said. "And I know I could, too. Let's go."

Troy hesitated. "You won't leave on your own again?" he asked Lakin. "You'll have Eli see you safely back to the cabin?"

She sighed but nodded.

"She said she would be careful," Parker said, as if vouching for her. Or maybe he was trying to convince himself.

He repeated the same words just a short while later when they settled on stools at the bar.

"What did Seller say that rattled you so much?" Troy asked. It was clear that Parker and Lakin had both been rattled.

"He just kept talking about her being single and the damn serial killer." Parker shuddered.

Troy grimaced. "I'm glad I mentioned him to Eli."

"I texted Eli, too, to check out the guy," Parker admitted.

"I thought he was a great customer for RTA," Troy said.

"You know I love my sister more than I care about business," Parker said.

Troy clasped the man's shoulder. "I know."

"What about you?"

"What do you mean?"

"She told me about the hotel, but it doesn't sound like you're doing it with her," Parker said.

"I…"

"I know you got hurt on the oil rig the last time you were gone," Parker said. "But that's just another reason you shouldn't go back."

"Wow, everyone's piling on today about that," Troy said. "My sister, apparently my mother and now you."

"You can understand why we all want you to stay in Shelby," Parker said. "Especially now."

Troy sighed. "With that serial killer and Jasper Whitlaw running around…"

"Jasper Whitlaw?" Parker asked. "Who's that?"

Troy grimaced again. "I thought Lakin or Eli might have told you."

"About this Whitlaw person?"

Troy nodded. "I guess I should have known Lakin wouldn't tell you."

"So Eli knows about him," Parker said. "But why wouldn't Lakin tell me?"

"Because she doesn't want your mom and dad to know," Troy said. "And I shouldn't have said anything."

"But now that you have, you're going to have to spill," Parker said.

"Eli knows more than I do," Troy said.

"That's why he's coming by the office to talk to Lakin," Parker said. "It's about Whitlaw."

Troy nodded. "Yeah…" And it was killing him to not be part of that conversation. He had to know exactly how dangerous Jasper Whitlaw was. "Maybe we should go back and make Eli tell us, too."

"You heard Lakin," Parker said. "She didn't want us there." He looked over at Troy, his brow wrinkled with suspicion. "What's going on with you two? She doesn't seem really happy with you."

"She's not," Troy admitted.

"And here I thought you would do anything to make her happy."

Anything but burden her with a cripple or with debt that he couldn't help her pay off. He remembered all too well how his mother had struggled after his dad died. He didn't want to put Lakin through that; he loved her too much.

Maybe he had to accept that he wasn't what would make her happy.

The boyfriend wasn't playing watchdog at the moment. Which was too bad because the gun lay on the seat next to him, and he couldn't wait to use it.

The boyfriend hadn't been around as much today as he usually was. When he was, he'd been with too many other people.

Unlike Lakin, who was alone right now. There wasn't another Colton anywhere around her as she sat alone in that office, watching the door, as if expecting someone to show up.

But he'd seen the others leave not long ago. The boyfriend and her brother were gone.

The others were as well.

She was all alone.

It was finally time to show little Miss Lakin just how much danger she was in...

# *Chapter 16*

Lakin waited and waited for Eli until she finally got a text from him.

Something came up. Will have to talk to you tomorrow.

What was the something that had come up? Had another body been found? Or maybe the serial killer?

She really hoped that was the case, so that nobody else would get hurt. Nobody else should lose their life or a loved one like her dad had lost so many people he cared about. She would have asked Eli why he couldn't make it, but too often he ignored questions like that. He had to keep the details of an investigation close to his chest so that things didn't get leaked to the press.

Despite his efforts, things did seem to be getting leaked.

Lakin understood why he had to be so secretive, but she would feel so much better if she knew what had come up. She would also feel so much better if she wasn't completely alone. But she was the one who'd shooed out Parker and Troy, so that she could talk to Eli without them present.

Now…

She could call either one of them, and they would rush back to her side. Still, she appreciated having a little distance from Troy, especially after last night.

She wanted to be with him again, wanted to sleep in his arms like she had the night before. She loved him so much, but she was pretty sure she was going to have to let him go when he went back to the oil rigs. After he'd been hurt, she would be terrified the entire time he was gone that he would be hurt again. She didn't want to live in fear of losing him. Or of losing herself.

That was how she felt right now, like she was losing part of herself. For so many years, it had been the two of them, loving and laughing and making plans for the future. But apparently she was the only one who really intended to follow through on those plans.

No. She wasn't going to live in fear for Troy or for anyone else. Seller had made her uneasy with his comments this morning, but she was not going to let him make her feel like a victim before anyone even tried to hurt her.

She'd already proven when she'd been abandoned at three years old that she was a survivor. She was strong.

She drew in a deep breath, stepped outside and locked the office door behind her. It was just a short distance from the office's porch to where her SUV was parked, but night had fallen like a black blanket. The porch light bore only a small hole in it. She pulled out her key fob and flashed her lights on, and that was when she saw *him*.

Not his face. But his height, his broadness. A man stood out in the darkness. Waiting for her…

With where he was standing between her and her SUV, she wouldn't be able to get into her vehicle. And if she turned around to unlock the office door, he might have time to run up and force his way inside with her before she could lock the door behind herself again.

She clicked her key fob again, turning on the vehicle alarm. Hopefully the blare of the horn and the blinking lights would draw a guest from their cabin or catch the attention of someone driving by.

She didn't wait around to find out. She ran.

The man ran after her; she could hear his feet pounding the ground behind her. She might have screamed, but she wasn't about to waste her breath. She needed all of it as she ran for her life.

Eli glanced at his phone to confirm that Lakin had read his text. She'd given it a thumbs-up because, of course, she would. She wouldn't argue with him and insist that he tell her what he'd found out about the man claiming to be her father, not like Troy would.

Or Kansas.

His cousin stood next to him in the lab, intently

watching the tech, Scott Montgomery, process the photograph. Since Eli had shared the situation with Kansas, she was as worried about Lakin as he was. She'd suggested they run more tests on the old snapshot.

"I'm sorry," Montgomery said. "I can't get enough DNA off the photograph to process, let alone compare it to anything left at the other crime scenes."

Kansas cursed.

Eli swallowed his. "Thanks for trying."

Scott nodded. "No problem. I really wish I was able to do more."

"We know," Kansas assured the man who smiled shyly back at her.

Eli figured the tech had a crush on her. But he suspected he wasn't the only man Eli worked with who had one on the beautiful state trooper.

"You really think this guy could be the serial killer?" Montgomery asked.

Eli shrugged. "I don't know. But I hope not." It would make sense, though, since the killings hadn't started until after Whitlaw's release from prison. That was why Eli had agreed with Kansas that the trip to the lab to try to pull DNA off the photograph was more important than meeting with Lakin. Eli could help her more by putting Whitlaw back in prison than by filling her in on what little he'd learned about the man.

But this trip to the lab hadn't given them any new

information and definitely no connection between Whitlaw and the Fiancée Killer.

As much as Eli wanted to find and stop the serial killer, he wasn't sure that he wanted it to be Whitlaw. The man was focused on Lakin right now. And not for the reason he claimed. What was his real connection to her?

More important, what did he really want from her?

Troy knew he shouldn't have left Lakin alone at the RTA office. When Parker got the text from Eli that he'd canceled on her, Troy rushed out of the bar and back to RTA. He didn't wait for Parker. He was too worried.

And for good reason. When he drove into the lot, he saw the lights flashing and heard the horn blaring on her SUV. Either someone had tried to break into it, or she had deliberately set off the alarm. Either way she was in trouble.

The second he threw open the door to his truck, he heard her scream. It chilled his blood. And then he started running.

She must be trying to get back to her cabin. He headed that way, yelling her name. He wasn't just calling out to let her know he was coming, but also to whoever might be chasing her.

Unless they'd already caught her...

He heard other running footsteps, but he couldn't see anything. Not even a star or a sliver of moon lit the way. What had happened to the lights in the other cabins? Were they all vacant?

"Lakin!" he called out again, trying to figure out where she was.

But she didn't call back to him. Was someone holding a hand over her mouth? Or was it worse than that?

"Lakin! The police are coming!" he yelled again. But he hadn't called them yet. Hopefully someone had who'd seen her lights flashing and heard her horn honking.

But if not...

There was no help coming but him. He had to find her.

It was too dark for him to track footprints unless he pulled out his phone. He heard no sirens in the distance. He needed to call the police himself.

He flashed his cell light on and immediately heard a gun cock. Then, seconds later, the blast of it being fired.

His first fear was for her, that Lakin had been shot.

But before he could call out to her, she screamed his name. Leaves rustled, and branches snapped near his head as bullets fired at him.

He ducked down, trying to take cover. It was clear whoever had been after her was willing or maybe even determined to kill him so that he didn't get in their way.

But he wasn't as worried about his life as he was hers. He had to figure out a way to stay alive and make sure that she did, too.

# *Chapter 17*

The person pursuing her had been so close that for a second Lakin had felt his breath on the back of her neck, his hand reaching for her hair. She'd screamed and ran harder, faster, more desperately because she hadn't thought anyone would hear her scream any more than they'd heard the blare of her vehicle alarm.

But then Troy had called out to her. She should have been relieved, but now she was afraid for both of them.

Instead of calling back with the man so close to her, she'd ducked under some low-hanging pine boughs. She held her breath, terrified.

Until she heard the gunshots.

She screamed Troy's name. But the shots weren't as close as she expected. Had the man turned around and gone back toward the office? Or had he gone after Troy instead?

Like the white knight he'd always been for her, Troy had rushed to her rescue, putting his own life in danger.

She didn't know what to do. If she ran from her

hiding place, she could get shot, too. And then she wouldn't be able to help Troy. If she turned on her phone, the light or the sound of it could give away her location. But she had to get help.

Pulling her RTA shirt out of her waistband, she concealed her phone inside it, then texted an SOS to her sibling/cousin group chat. Her fingers were trembling so badly that all she managed was in fact SOS. She couldn't text that she was afraid Troy was hurt.

That he might have been shot...

She didn't even want to think it, as if putting her fear into words would somehow make it come true.

Tears burned her eyes, and so many regrets rushed through her. She'd been so frustrated with him since he'd come back, so disappointed with his stubbornness. She'd wasted so much time being angry when she could have been with him like she'd been last night. Like she wanted to be now, wrapped up in his strong arms, feeling his heart beating against hers.

Was his heart still beating? Was Troy alive?

Or had one of those gunshots stopped his heart? If it had, Lakin suspected hers would stop, too.

The SOS scared the crap out of Kansas. It wasn't like Lakin to ask for help ever. Not even back when she was being bullied in school. She'd just ignored the bullies until one of her brothers or Kansas or the Amoses had put a stop to it. Of all of them, Troy had been the most effective at ending the bullying.

Where was he that Lakin had sent out an SOS?

He was back from the oil rigs, so he should have been where he usually was when he was in Shelby, at Lakin's side.

"Can't you drive any faster?" she asked Eli, even though he probably already had the accelerator pressed to the floorboards of his ABI SUV.

He didn't even spare her a glance. Was he mad at her? If she hadn't talked him into the trip to the lab, he would have been here with Lakin, protecting her from whatever compelled her to send that SOS text.

"Scott really thought he might be able to get something off the photograph," she said. "And if this Whitlaw guy is the Fiancée Killer…" He was even more dangerous than they'd thought.

And he was out there, somewhere in Shelby, stalking Lakin.

Kansas swore, then added, "I'm really sorry."

Eli still didn't say anything, but a muscle twitched in his cheek from how tightly he'd clenched his jaw. And Kansas knew if something happened to Lakin, Eli wasn't going to forgive her any more than she was going to forgive herself.

As they neared RTA, other sirens blared and lights flashed. Kansas had called the local police, knowing that they would reach the location given for Lakin's cell sooner than she and Eli would. But it wasn't just the local police already on the scene, an ambulance was as well. Had someone been hurt? Kansas prayed that it wasn't Lakin. But if not her, who? So much of their family worked at RTA. Even her dad and her uncle stopped by frequently despite having "retired" from the adventure business they'd started when they first moved to Shelby. When they'd fled from family tragedy to start over.

But had family tragedy found them again?

Troy flinched as the EMT pressed something against the stinging skin on his cheek. He wasn't sure if a bullet had grazed his face or one of the tree branches he'd jumped into for cover. But he didn't care about himself.

"Are you really all right?" he asked Lakin again. He tried to see her around the paramedic treating Troy in the back of the ambulance.

Once the emergency vehicles had pulled into the parking lot of RTA, the shooting had stopped, and Troy wasn't the only one who'd rushed out of a hiding place. Fortunately Lakin had been hiding, too.

"Like I already told you, I'm fine," she said. "He never took any shots at *me*. I didn't even know he had a gun until I heard the shooting start."

"Who was it?" Kansas asked just as Bobby Reynolds opened his mouth. Probably to ask the same thing. Clearly Lakin's cousin and brother weren't willing to leave this investigation in the officer's hands.

Lakin shook her head. "I never saw more than a shadow. He was standing by my SUV when I clicked my key fob to unlock it. Then I set off the alarm."

"That was smart," Kansas said.

"But then I couldn't see anything with the lights flashing," Lakin said.

"You couldn't tell if it was Jasper Whitlaw?" Eli asked, appearing beside Kansas.

"Where were you?" Troy asked the ABI lieutenant. "I wouldn't have left her if you hadn't said you were meeting her at the office."

"That was my fault," Kansas said. "I thought one of our techs could get DNA off that photograph, but he wasn't able to after all."

"So he couldn't get any DNA to see if it matches…" Lakin said, her voice soft with obvious disappointment.

"He's not your father," Eli said.

She nodded. "I know that Dad is—"

"That's not what I meant," Eli interrupted her. "He can't be your biological father because he was in prison for assault. He was serving a two-year sentence during the time you would have been conceived and born."

"He's been in prison," Troy said, his gut churning with fear for Lakin. Just as he'd suspected, the man was dangerous as well as a liar.

Eli nodded. "More than once. He's been in and out a lot for assault. And he just got out recently."

"And came looking for me," Lakin remarked. "Why? Since I'm not his daughter, what does he want?"

"I don't know," Eli said.

Troy had an idea. Money. But when he'd mentioned that before, Lakin had gotten upset with him. And he didn't want her to be upset with him again, especially not when they'd come so close to losing their lives.

"What are you going to do to keep her safe is the real question," Troy said.

"We don't know that the person who shot at you is Jasper Whitlaw," Eli pointed out.

Troy had given the lieutenant some other potential suspects. But he couldn't see Billy Hoover waiting all these years before trying to take him out. Unless he was so damn drunk he wasn't thinking straight. And Seller...

Did a guy as rich as that do his own dirty work? And why would he go after Troy anyway? Why would anyone? Unless it was just because he was in their way, standing between them and Lakin.

Harrison's threat rang in his ears again, about losing more than his job if he went through with the lawsuit. Had he been talking about Troy's life?

But the shooter had been waiting in the parking lot for Lakin, trying to get her alone. Well, if anyone knew Troy at all, they would know that it would hurt him more if Lakin was hurt. Hell, it would destroy him.

"We have to make sure Lakin is safe," Troy said.

"You're the one who nearly got shot," Lakin pointed out. "You need protection, too."

He needed her. He needed to close his arms around

her and never let her go. But he wasn't sure that would keep either of them safe.

"We'll keep an officer in the area," Reynolds said.

"We'll be close, too," Eli said, gesturing toward him and Kansas.

Reynolds nodded. He probably knew better than to argue with a Colton. When one of them was in danger, they were going to rally around their loved one.

Troy was counting on that. He wasn't doing a very damn good job on his own keeping Lakin safe. But he definitely wasn't going to leave her side from now on, either.

He told her as much when they were finally escorted safely inside her cabin.

Instead of the pushback he expected, she linked her arms around his neck and hugged him. Then she pulled back and touched his face below the bandage on his cheek.

"Never leaving my side isn't safe or practical," she said. "You could have been killed tonight."

"And here everybody has been worrying about me working on the oil rigs," he said. "I've been in more danger since coming back to Shelby."

"But all you have so far is a scratch," she said. "You were hospitalized from working on the oil rig."

Hospitalized and paralyzed. The fear of feeling that helpless ever again never left him. Though he'd nearly felt that helpless tonight when he hadn't known where she was or if she was safe.

"I was so worried about you," he admitted. "When

I saw the alarm going off on your vehicle and then I heard you scream…" He shuddered as he relived those moments.

She hugged him again. "I'm safe, Troy."

For now. "I'm going to do everything I can to make sure you stay that way," he assured her.

"So now you're my bodyguard?"

He nodded. "Until you're no longer in danger."

"We're safe here," she said. "You know there are officers and troopers outside watching the cabin."

Troy stepped back. "So you don't want me close?"

"I want you even closer," she said with a smile. She entwined her fingers with his and tugged him through the open bedroom door.

His pulse quickened almost to the speed it had been when he'd heard her scream. He'd been so afraid that he'd lost her. But she was here, with him. Safe.

But he was still so afraid he was going to lose her. Maybe not to a killer, but to his own stubbornness. "I love you, Lakin," he said.

And he waited for her to say it again. But she kissed him instead, her mouth moving over his. As she kissed him, she undressed him.

Once he was naked, she dropped to her knees and closed her lips around his shaft. He groaned, and she lifted her head. "Are you all right?"

"No," he said.

"Where are you hurt?"

"I ache," he said.

She jumped up from the floor. "Do I need to call the paramedics back?"

He shook his head. "You're the only one who can relieve this pain," he said.

"Oh…" She smiled as she realized what he was saying.

"I need you so badly." His entire body was filled with a tension only she could relieve. But he didn't want her to do it with her mouth. He wanted to be inside her, part of her.

He undressed her, baring every silky inch of her skin for his touch and his taste. He ran his lips and his tongue over her breasts and then lower.

Her knees buckled, and she dropped back onto the bed, pulling him down with her. He rolled over so that he wouldn't crush her, but Lakin wasn't small or delicate. She was strong, and she pushed him onto his back and straddled him. Then she guided his cock inside her, and it was like coming home.

She moaned and bit her lip. Then she began to move with frantic urgency, as if she was as desperate for release as he was. He reached up and cupped her breasts in his hands.

She leaned down, her dark hair falling like a curtain around them as she kissed him. Their mouths mated like their bodies.

He stroked his thumbs over her nipples. She moaned again and moved faster, rocking back and forth, sliding up and down, driving him out of his mind. Then she came, her inner muscles convulsing around him, squeezing his cock.

She screamed his name. His body tensed, and finally his release came. He thrust his hips up, filling her as she filled his heart with the love he felt for her.

He didn't dare express it again, afraid that she wouldn't say it back. That she couldn't. Maybe she didn't love him anymore, or at least not like she once had when she could see a future for them. Their business, a family... All the dreams she'd had for their life together... He'd taken them away from her with his unwillingness to commit.

And tonight someone else had nearly taken his life. Had the shooter been after him or her?

He must have tensed up again because she wrapped her arms around him and murmured, "Go to sleep. We're safe here."

He was worried they wouldn't be safe anywhere from whoever was after them. Was it Jasper Whitlaw? Someone else? Someone who might be even more dangerous, like the Fiancée Killer?

# *Chapter 18*

Lakin should have been exhausted, but maybe there was just too much adrenaline coursing through her body. From the close call she and Troy had had and from how they'd made love again. While he'd fallen asleep afterward, she lay awake next to him, listening to his even breathing and the beat of his heart beneath her cheek.

She loved him so much even when he frustrated her with his stubbornness. But was he the only one being stubborn?

She'd thought she didn't want him leaving again because she didn't want him getting hurt on the oil rigs, but as he pointed out, he'd been hurt here, too. Was his safety just an excuse she was using because she wanted him with her?

She did want him with her. Always. But she also didn't want him getting hurt, and in trying to protect her like he had tonight, he had been. The bandage on his chiseled cheekbone made her feel queasy with regret and fear.

Her cell vibrated against the bedside table with

an incoming call. Not wanting to wake up Troy, she grabbed it from the nightstand and slipped out of bed. Maybe it was one of her siblings calling. Or one of the officers watching the cabin.

But when she stepped out of the bedroom and looked down at the number, she recognized the one Jasper Whitlaw had scrawled on the back of the photograph.

He wasn't her father, but why had he been in that picture with her and her biological mother?

Wanting answers, she slid her finger across the screen to accept the call, but she couldn't bring herself to say anything. She had no idea what to say. Even if she asked the questions she had for him, she doubted he would tell her the truth.

"Hey, little girl," he greeted her. He sounded amused. Was this all some sick joke to him?

"I know you're not my father," she told him.

He snorted. "What? You trying to pretend you're really a Colton now?"

"I am," she said. "But I know you were in prison around the time I would have been conceived and born. You're nothing to me."

"I'm a link to your mother," he said. "If you want to know the truth about her…"

Her heart yearned for the truth, to know more about the woman she looked so much like. The woman who had left her in that grocery store all those years ago.

"I'll find her on my own," she said. That way

she would trust what she found out. She wouldn't be hearing it from a man who'd already lied to her.

"You won't find her," he said.

A heaviness settled on Lakin's heart. She was dead. That had to be what he meant. But again she didn't trust him for the truth. "I'm not going to pay you for information on her," she warned him. "So if you're after money, you're not going to get any out of me."

"Then maybe I will go to your Colton daddy," Jasper threatened. "Or maybe I'll go straight to the press. They buy stories. They might be interested in one about a serial killer stalking Shelby, Alaska, the way Caroline Colton was stalked and murdered years ago along with her parents. I'm sure the press would love to dig up that family tragedy, probably set up their vans and stuff right outside Will and Sasha Colton's house. It's a nice one. I can make sure they find it like I did."

So he had been outside their house that day. Had he also driven Troy off the road?

"Stay away from my parents," she said. "And don't go to the press."

"Why?" he asked, as if he was only idly curious. "Are you going to make it worth my while?"

"I… I…" Lakin had no money of her own anymore. She'd put it all into the hotel. She couldn't go to her dad for more, not for this. Not for blackmail.

"I'll get some money," she said. But what she really intended was to get Eli and Kansas to track down and arrest the blackmailer. They would probably have to have a recording of him actually blackmailing her, though, so it was more than her word against his.

"It better be more than I can get from the press for selling this story," he threatened.

"It will be." She wished she'd been recording this call. If only that had occurred to her sooner... "Where do I find you when I get the money together?" she asked.

"Since all you've given me was forty bucks, I've been camping outside, not far from your place," he said. "I couldn't afford a hotel."

From the way he said *hotel*, she wondered if he knew about the Shelby Hotel. Had he been there that day the window was broken? He had to be the one who'd been stalking her. He knew too much, like where her parents lived. It made her sick that she might have been the one who led him to them.

"Were you here tonight?" she asked. "Did you shoot at Troy?"

He snorted. "Why would I shoot at anyone, girl? That's not going to get me what I want, which is money enough to start over somewhere. And since I'm still on probation, I can't have a firearm. It wasn't me."

What he said made sense but also made her more uneasy. If not him, who had taken those shots at Troy and why?

"Where can I find you?" she asked.

He named a road that had a riverbank on one side

where people often camped. He probably wasn't alone out there. She would make certain that *she* wasn't alone when she met him.

But she was also going to make sure Troy wasn't with her or anywhere near her. She didn't want him putting his life in danger trying to keep her safe.

Troy jerked awake, imagining he felt that sting against his cheek all over again. But it was just a dull throb, unlike his pulse that was suddenly racing when he realized he was alone in bed.

"Lakin!" he called out.

Maybe she was just in the bathroom. But he jumped out of bed to find it and the rest of the cabin empty. She was gone.

He didn't think she would have headed to the office this early. Dawn had only lightened the sky a bit; the sun had yet to rise. So where was she?

He grabbed his cell and called her, but her voicemail immediately picked up. She either wasn't taking his call or she couldn't.

He called Eli next. "You're supposed to have someone watching Lakin. Do you know where she is?" He braced himself for Eli to point out that Troy had said he was watching her. He already felt so damn guilty for falling asleep. More than once she'd slipped out of the cabin without him noticing. Good thing he wasn't a real bodyguard.

"She called me," Eli said. "And told me where she's headed."

"Where?" Troy asked. But part of him already knew and dreaded what her brother was about to tell him.

"To meet Jasper Whitlaw," Eli confirmed his worst fear.

"Why the hell would she do that?" They'd told her the man was dangerous. He'd been in and out of prison for assault for years.

"He threatened our family," Eli said.

Troy knew Lakin would do anything to protect the family she loved so much. He cursed.

"I'm on my way to catch up with her," Eli said. "She can't have much of a head start. She called me just a few minutes ago."

Hopefully she didn't have much of a head start on Troy either then. "Where?" he asked. "Where is she meeting him?"

"She didn't wake you up because she doesn't want you getting shot again," Eli said. "So I'm not going to be the one who puts you in danger."

"No, you're not," Troy agreed. "I am."

But he realized he didn't need Eli's help to find her. He disconnected the call.

Years ago, he and Lakin had shared their phone locations with each other. Because he was out of cellular range so much when he was working on the oil rigs, he had nearly forgotten. He checked it now.

A little dot blinked within a circle close to a riverbank just a short distance from RTA.

He would be able to find her. Hopefully he

wouldn't be too late to help her. Because he didn't think Jasper Whitlaw was just a threat to her family.

He was a threat to her, too.

He'd put fear in her; he knew and relished that fear. Now all he had to do was wait. When people were afraid, they didn't think rationally. They were too emotional, too panicked, to think clearly. To make a plan.

Like the plan he'd made.

The plan he was going to carry out so that he would finally get what was owed to him.

And so would the Coltons.

# Chapter 19

Lakin knew she was taking a risk sneaking out on her own, but she didn't want Troy to get hurt again. She didn't want her family hurt, either, but she had called Eli for help. She glanced at her phone, checking the time. He should have been here already.

He'd told her to wait for him before she got out of her vehicle, but she was impatient. She needed to record Jasper Whitlaw's threats and extortion attempt. Then she could use that to make him leave Shelby and her family in peace. She couldn't wait any longer for her brother. Maybe he was already here. He'd told her that he would stay out of sight so Whitlaw wouldn't know he was there.

But where was Whitlaw?

Lakin walked around the area where he claimed to be camping, but she didn't see even a place where a sleeping bag might have lain let alone remains of a fire. It got cold at night in September. Maybe he was sleeping in his truck and just parking it here.

But she didn't even see any tire tracks.

Had he lied to her?

But why? She couldn't give him the money she'd promised him if she couldn't find him.

Had he realized she was lying and trying to set him up? That would explain why he'd given her a phony location.

She might have been relieved that he wasn't here if she wasn't more worried about where he might be. Had he accosted her dad like he had her? Was he trying to get money directly from the Coltons? Why did he seem to resent them for adopting her anyway? She'd been abandoned. It wasn't like Whitlaw or anyone else had wanted her but the Coltons.

And eventually Troy had wanted her, too. Or so she'd thought. Of course, now she wasn't as confident of having a future with him as she had been. Actually, after the shooting last night, she wasn't as confident of having a future at all.

But nobody had been shooting at her. They'd been shooting at Troy. Was he the real target in all of this?

She'd left him back at the cabin, alone and asleep and completely vulnerable.

What the hell had she been thinking? Could she get back to him in time to make sure that he was safe? Or was she already too late?

Troy jumped in his truck and headed right where he thought Lakin was. But once he was away from the Wi-Fi of the cabin, her location disappeared, and he wasn't able to pull up cellular data either. He had no bars out here; the tower was too far away. So he had no idea where she was, just where she'd been.

Wandering around the riverbank where he'd pinpointed her location earlier, he wasn't even sure where he was.

Why would Lakin have met Whitlaw here? Or Eli? Wasn't Eli supposed to be coming as her backup, to make sure she stayed safe? Had the ABI lieutenant let her down again?

A branch snapped behind Troy, and he whirled around with his fists up to defend himself. They were his only weapon.

But the gun that faced him wasn't the one that fired at him the night before. Eli immediately holstered his weapon when he saw Troy.

"Of course you wouldn't stay away like I told you to," Eli remarked.

"Of course I wouldn't," Troy agreed. "Not that there is anything or anyone to stay away from. Have you seen Lakin or Whitlaw?"

Eli shook his head. "I saw some tire tracks, but they appear to be from only one vehicle. Probably Lakin's SUV."

"Not Whitlaw's truck," Troy said. "Why would he tell her to meet him here?"

"Maybe he knew what she was up to," Eli remarked. "And wasn't going to fall for it."

"What was she up to?" Troy asked. "Why would she agree to meet him? She has no money to give him." She'd invested it all in the hotel. Troy would have given her money if she'd asked, though…and if he'd thought that was really all that Whitlaw wanted. But now, knowing Whitlaw wasn't her father, he had a feeling the man had a whole other agenda where Lakin was concerned.

"She was going to record him demanding money in exchange for keeping his mouth shut to the press about my family. If she could get him to admit to that, I could arrest him for extortion," Eli explained.

Troy chuckled for a moment at her brilliance. She was going to turn the tables on an ex-con. But then his amusement dried up. "So where is she?"

"I don't know," Eli said. "I had to take a detour around a logging truck that lost some of its load in the road. So I was late getting here."

"But like you pointed out, there is only one set of tire tracks here," Troy said. "Whitlaw drives an old truck. His tread marks would have been bigger and deeper than Lakin's."

Eli nodded. "He was never here."

"I don't get why he would have told her to meet him here even if he knew what she was up to," Troy said. "Why this place?" He glanced around at the river and the trees surrounding them.

"I don't know," Eli murmured. "Maybe he wanted her away from the cabin. Or away from someone else."

Troy's stomach muscles clenched with dread. "I don't like this."

"Me, neither," Eli agreed. "He was threatening to go public with my family tragedy."

Troy sucked in a breath. "When you said family, I didn't think about your aunt and grandparents' murders. How did he find out about that? And no wonder Lakin agreed to meet him and pay him off." With money she didn't have. But maybe she would have gone to the same person she'd gone to for the hotel. "Call your dad," he suggested. "See if he's heard from her."

"I don't think she wants him to know what's going on," Eli said.

Troy suspected she wasn't the only one who didn't want to worry their father. But he knew how much Will and Sasha Colton loved their daughter. "He's going to want to know," he pointed out. He'd realized too late how many people he'd hurt because he hadn't reached out when he was injured. "The people who love you want to show up for you."

Eli groaned. "You're right."

Troy took no comfort from that. He wasn't going to feel better until he knew where Lakin was and that she was safe. "While you call him, I'm going to head back to the cabin. She probably would have gone back there or the office."

Eli reached out and squeezed his shoulder. "Be careful."

Troy nodded. He wasn't worried about himself; he was worried about her. She'd agreed to meet with a dangerous ex-con in order to protect her family. She didn't care about her own safety at all.

And finally he could relate to how she felt when he went off to work the oil rigs, doing the same job that had killed his father, knowingly putting himself in danger just as she had done in agreeing to meet Whitlaw.

Troy had to find her before something happened to her. She was the most amazing person, so kind and loving and supportive to everyone. Troy had failed her in so many ways; he just wanted to have the chance to make it up to her.

Will hated getting calls this early in the morning because they were rarely good news. At least it hadn't woken him up; he'd already been out for his run and was just opening the back door when his cell vibrated.

Sasha was awake, too, in the kitchen. He could hear the pots and pans and smell the coffee brewing. But he stepped back outside to answer the call.

"Good morning, Eli. Or at least I hope it is."

The hesitation was all the confirmation Will needed that there was nothing good about this morning.

Then Eli asked, "Have you seen Lakin today?"

Will's stomach pitched a bit, and he was glad it was still empty. "No. Is there any reason she would have been by so early? Why are you looking for her?"

"Uh, it's just…"

Eli's breath of relief rattled his phone. "Never mind. Troy texted that her phone location shows she's back at her cabin."

"What's going on, son?" Will demanded.

"We'll bring you up to speed soon," Eli promised, and he ended the call before Will could argue.

What the hell was going on? When Lakin stopped by a few days ago, she'd seemed tense and distracted. She'd kept looking out the window, almost as if she thought she was being followed.

His skin chilled at the thought of his daughter having a stalker like Caroline had. Nobody had believed that man was dangerous until it was too late.

Until too many lives had been lost...

That couldn't be the case with Lakin. Will could not let that be the case because he couldn't lose any more of his family than he already had.

Lakin had to be safe.

# *Chapter 20*

When Lakin pulled up to the cabin, Troy's truck was gone. That meant he'd driven off somewhere, and she could imagine where: to find her.

Sneaking off without him wasn't going to keep him safe, especially if he'd been the target all along. She knew he'd talked to her brother Mitch about what happened on the oil rig. Maybe the lawyer had talked to the company and they'd sent someone to shut Troy up. After all, a dead man couldn't sue them. Not that she was sure he was having Mitch sue for him or just to make the workplace safer.

Troy *should* sue them for his pain and suffering. But when Troy's mother had sued the company, the case had been dismissed. Now it had cost her a husband and very nearly a son as well. Lakin wanted to make sure that Mrs. Amos didn't lose that son here in Shelby, either.

Even though it didn't look like he was in the cabin, Lakin headed inside to see if he'd left a note. Although he probably would have texted instead. She reached for her cell as she approached the door, but finding it partially open distracted her. Since his truck wasn't here, she assumed that Troy had left in such a hurry that he hadn't closed it tightly.

She needed to find out where he was. She unlocked her phone as she pushed open the door to the empty cabin.

But it wasn't empty. There was the acrid smell of cigarette smoke, so thick that someone had to still be inside. She backed toward the front door, but it banged into her.

Before she could whirl around to see who had been hiding behind the door, a hand covered her nose and mouth with a cloth and blocked her vision. Another smell, cloying and syrupy, filled her nose, smothering in its sweetness.

She tried to wrest herself away, but a strong arm encircled her, keeping her arms locked to her sides. As the smell overwhelmed her, consciousness began to fade. Her phone slipped through her fingers and dropped to the floor.

Then her legs buckled, and she dropped to the floor as well. She blinked, trying to clear her vision, but before she could focus on the face of the intruder, the last of her consciousness slipped away.

Once Troy had driven a short distance away from the riverbank, he'd been able to pull up Lakin's location again. She'd gone back to the cabin, so he texted Eli to let him know. Unfortunately when he pulled off the road to send that text, a tractor had managed to get ahead of him. A very slow-moving tractor.

When he was finally able to pass it, he worried that Lakin might leave the cabin again before he got back to her. Instead of checking his cell again, he pressed harder on the accelerator until he was speeding down the lane to her cabin.

He breathed a sigh of relief when he saw her SUV parked near the porch. She was still home.

And that was what she was to him: home. His heart, where he always wanted to be, was here in her cabin on RTA property or in the old Shelby Hotel. Suite Home would be a sweet home for them.

Eager to tell her that and confirm that she was really all right, Troy pushed open his driver's door and nearly sprinted up to the porch.

But when he neared the door and found it partially open, his heart started beating even faster. He drew in a breath, inhaling something unusual, cloying and chemical at the same time. He coughed, cleared his throat, then yelled, "Lakin!"

His shout echoed off the wood walls and floor. There was no response. Outside not even a bird chirped or a leaf rustled. She was gone.

He wanted to believe that she'd walked to the office, but she wouldn't have left without closing and locking the cabin door. And then there was that smell...

That chemical smell and a lingering odor of cigarette smoke.

When he stepped through the open door, he saw a big handkerchief lying on the floor. Was that where the smell was coming from?

He didn't touch it. He didn't dare because he had a feeling Lakin's home had just become a crime scene. But what was the crime? Abduction? Or worse?

He couldn't let himself think that. He couldn't let himself believe that he wouldn't see Lakin again, or he would become as paralyzed as when he fell from the oil rig. He wouldn't be able to breathe, let alone move.

He had to find her.

The search and rescue team had just gotten a call. Another woman was missing. The last woman who'd gone missing from the Shelby area had turned up just a few days ago. Dead. Dawn Ellis.

This woman could not turn up the same way. This woman was family. Kansas drew in a deep breath, trying to pull herself together, for her family's sake and mostly for Lakin's. She had to find her cousin.

So she rallied the search and rescue team. This had to be a rescue, not a recovery. They had to find Lakin.

Alive.

# *Chapter 21*

Lakin was stuck in an old nightmare. The one where she could hear voices shouting at each other. She'd had such a hard time for so long with raised voices. School had been so tough in the beginning until she'd learned to ignore her reaction and suppress the old memories.

But they were back now, pulling her into the nightmare. The shouts. The sharp slap of skin against skin. Someone was fighting.

And the crying…

Someone was hurt.

Tears burned the back of her throat, like they were running down behind her closed eyes. Behind her closed eyes, images wavered, faded and yellowed like that old photograph Jasper Whitlaw had given her.

He wasn't her father.

But she heard her father's voice now: Will's deep rumble. He used to wake her up from the nightmares and hold her until she stopped crying and trembling.

She needed him now.

She needed Troy to rush to her rescue like he always did. She imagined she felt like he had after falling off the oil rig—she couldn't move. She couldn't even open her eyes. She couldn't pull herself out of the nightmare.

She had to…

She couldn't keep counting on other people to rescue her. Especially not Troy. He wasn't sticking around. He would go back to those damn oil rigs, back to putting his life in danger. Maybe it was better being in danger doing a job than defending her. She didn't want him getting shot at again. She didn't want him or anyone else to risk their life for hers because she wouldn't be able to live with the guilt of causing someone else harm.

She had to rally her strength. And she also had to clear her head enough that she would be able to figure out who the hell had grabbed her and what they wanted with her. Then she had to get the hell away from them.

She drew in a little shaky breath and managed to lift her heavy lids. Not much… Just enough to see that she was in some kind of cave. Walls of rock surrounded her. The dirt was cold and hard beneath her body. The ground wasn't smooth, either; rocks and twigs poked into her back.

She tried to move her hands, but they were numb, the circulation cut off from duct tape binding her wrists tightly together.

There was duct tape around her ankles, too.

And over her mouth…

She couldn't move. She couldn't speak, and in the dimness of that cave, she really couldn't see, either. But she knew, from the rumble of voices, that she wasn't alone. Had more than one person abducted her? Was more than one holding her here? Or was it just one person on the phone?

A sudden flash of light illuminated a corner of the cave. The light was from a phone. She could see its screen but not the face of the person holding it. Once again, he was only a shadow looming in the darkness, like the monster she used to imagine lurked in her closet or under her bed.

Now she knew that the monster was real.

Troy kept his phone app open, looking for an update on Lakin's location. But her last location still showed the cabin from nearly an hour ago.

"Why do we have to wait for search and rescue?" Troy asked. Eli had shown up soon after Troy at the cabin. But it hadn't mattered; they'd both been too late to save Lakin from being abducted. "You and I should be able to follow the tracks."

"Do you want to waste your time?" Eli asked. "We don't know if she was dragged off to a vehicle or…" He choked as if he couldn't even say the words.

Was he going to say what Troy was afraid to even consider? That she'd been partially buried like those other women?

"She could have been put in a vehicle," Eli said. "And if they're not on foot, they could be anywhere.

We have to wait for the dogs to see if they can follow a scent."

Troy understood that, but waiting was killing him. It was like those weeks he'd lain in the hospital bed unable to move, to feel anything but fear and panic. He'd hated that helplessness.

He hated even more that someone had taken Lakin.

"Where are they?" he asked, his voice gruff with the fear choking him. He felt as if he couldn't breathe, like he'd hit the water again after a long fall.

Eli shrugged. "I don't know where the team is, but they should be here soon."

Troy realized Lakin's brother was as frustrated and frightened as he was. Maybe more so because he'd seen what had happened to the other women who'd disappeared.

"This isn't the serial killer, is it?" Troy asked, although he'd been reluctant to even consider that horrific possibility. "This has to be Whitlaw. Or maybe that rich RTA client. Or Billy Hoover." But any of them might also be the serial killer. His stomach pitched, bile rising with the terrifying thought.

"It's not doing either of us any good with you speculating about what's happened," Eli said, his voice gruff with emotion. "We just need to stay calm."

When the person who mattered most to him was in danger? Possible grave danger? Troy was hanging on to his sanity the best he could at the moment. Calmness was out of the question.

"If the SAR team doesn't get here soon, I'm going to start looking myself," he warned Eli.

"And potentially contaminate the scene and the dogs' ability to track?" Eli shook his head. "You don't think I want to be out there myself, looking for my sister? I know I have to follow protocol."

Troy didn't have to; he wasn't in law enforcement. But he also didn't want to do anything that might lower their chances of finding Lakin alive.

Eli totally understood and shared Troy's frustration. Where the hell was search and rescue? They had to get the damn dogs here before the scent went cold. Before they lost their chance to find his sister.

Troy was right; maybe they needed to just start looking for her themselves.

Eli's cell vibrated in his pocket. Maybe it was Kansas, calling with an updated ETA. But when he glanced at his screen it was lit up with: Dad.

Eli was tempted to swipe Ignore. But he couldn't help but wonder about the timing of his dad's call. Had someone notified their parents that Lakin was missing? If so, Dad had to be as out of his mind with fear as Eli and Troy.

He clicked to accept. "Dad—"

"Eli, I just got a ransom call for Lakin."

"What?"

"You told me she was home," Will reminded him. "So I wanted to check with you—"

"She's not here," Eli interjected. "Troy got back

to the cabin and found the door open. Her SUV is here, but she isn't."

"And?" Will asked because he had to know there was more.

"Troy found a rag with chloroform on it," Eli admitted. It was the only way someone could have taken Lakin without her managing to get away like she had the other night when someone accosted her outside the office. She hadn't had to fight hard that night, though; she'd just had to run until Troy showed up.

But Troy hadn't been fast enough to save her this time, and Eli could tell it was killing him. Troy paced, his limp all but forgotten, as he waited for the SAR team.

"Did you get to talk to her, Dad?" Eli asked.

"No."

"Any proof that this person who called actually has her?"

"No," his father admitted. "But I don't care. I'm going to get the money together that they want, so I will be ready when they call back to tell me where to leave that money."

"Dad…" Eli wanted to warn him that it wouldn't guarantee her safe return. Nothing would. But his dad knew that as well as he did. "You have to make sure that you get to talk to her when the person calls back. What did the caller sound like?"

"A man. I couldn't tell his age or anything by his

voice, though, and the phone number was blocked," his dad said.

"I'll have your records checked," Eli said. "We might be able to get it unblocked." Montgomery might know a way. The crime-scene tech was very savvy.

"You do what you have to do to get our girl back," Will said. "And so will I."

Eli's blood chilled. He'd never heard his dad sound so determined. But he knew why; he didn't want to lose Lakin like he'd lost his younger sister. Aunt Caroline.

Before he could say anything else, Dad disconnected the call.

"What is it?" Troy asked.

"My dad just got a ransom call."

Troy cursed.

"No, this could be good news," Eli said. "There were no ransom calls when those other women were abducted."

"So you don't think it's the Fiancée Killer who has her?" Troy asked. He sounded a little more hopeful now as he stopped pacing and studied Eli's face.

Eli nodded. But just because it wasn't the serial killer who had her didn't mean she wasn't still in danger. He knew that; he just wanted to assuage some of Troy's fear and his own. But he wouldn't be sure of anything until they found Lakin. They had to find her.

Eli had been in law enforcement long enough to

know how few kidnapping victims were ever recovered alive.

Lakin had to be the exception to that grim statistic, though. They had to be able to get her back safely. And soon.

# *Chapter 22*

Lakin closed her eyes, pretending to be asleep when the shadow moved from the corner of the cave over to where she lay. She knew it was best to not see the face of her abductor. He was more likely to let her go if she couldn't identify him.

That was her father's voice she'd heard in her dream. It had been coming from this man's cell phone. There was only one probable reason for that: a ransom call.

Dad had already loaned her so much money. She didn't want him paying out more for her. She definitely didn't want him to pay it only for her not to be released.

She intended to release herself, though. She'd managed to roll to her side and get one of those twigs near her wrists. She would be able to use the sharp end that had been jabbing into her back to fray the duct tape. If the man left her alone…

He stood for a long moment over her. Then he murmured, "Like looking at a damn ghost…"

Her skin chilled, goose bumps rising as she recognized the voice and simultaneously what he meant. Her birth mother was definitely dead. He wouldn't have called Lakin a ghost if she wasn't.

She schooled her features to remain relaxed, her breathing deep and easy. Finally he stepped over her. She lifted one lid just a fraction of an inch and watched as he exited the cave, which suddenly seemed brighter without Jasper Whitlaw inside it.

He was the dark shadow. The person who'd been stalking her. Just for money? Or was that nightmare about shouting and slapping and crying more than a dream? Could it be a memory? One Whitlaw might not want her to remember again.

Had she been there when her mother died?

In that case, even if her father paid him the ransom he demanded, Whitlaw might not have any intention of releasing her. She had to act fast.

She grabbed the stick and contorted her body so she could tear through the tape around her ankles. Then she wedged the sharp tip back between her wrists and managed to tear through the tape binding them as well. Once her hands were free, she reached up and eased the tape from her mouth, swallowing the cry of pain that wanted to slip out as the tape pulled at her skin and her lips.

She didn't want to alert Whitlaw that she was free. But she wasn't actually free yet. She pushed herself up from the ground, but her legs were shaky, and dizziness had black spots dancing before her eyes.

She blinked and steadied herself, then moved to the mouth of the cave.

He was standing out there, near a battered old truck parked in a stand of pines. She hadn't seen that truck at the cabin when she came home earlier. Had it already been parked here? How had he managed to get it through the thick forest of trees that covered this side of the mountain? Was this the mountain behind RTA? Was she close to home?

She tried to consider which direction to go, but again dizziness threatened to overwhelm her. She really didn't have time to think. The man was just standing there smoking. If he turned and saw her...

She slipped out of the cave and started moving as quietly as she could away from him and that truck. Holding even her breath so that she wouldn't alert him, she placed each foot softly against the ground. But a twig snapped beneath the sole of her hiking boot.

He whirled toward her. "Damn it, girl. Stop! Stop right now, or I'll shoot you!"

She did the opposite. She ran like she had that night he'd been waiting for her outside the office.

She knew now that it had to have been him that night. He'd lied when he told her on the phone that he didn't have a gun. But of course she shouldn't have expected him to tell her the truth about anything. The man was a liar and probably a killer as well.

"You are just like your worthless mama, girl," he shouted as he ran after her. "No matter how many times Stella ran from me, I always caught that faithless wife of mine." He coughed, probably from all his smoking and the exertion of running. "I'm going to catch you, too, and then I'm going to kill you like I did her, like I would have killed you all those years ago if she hadn't dumped you in that grocery store."

Tears stung her eyes. Her mother hadn't abandoned her; she'd saved her. She must have already been wounded when she'd left her at the grocery store.

"Before I could find you, social services got involved, and then those damn Coltons adopted you," he said, his breathing getting more labored as he chased after her.

Her lungs burned with the need for more air as she wound higher up the mountain. Her feet slipped on rocks and sand, and she clutched at tree branches to pull herself up.

But he was so close that she could still hear everything he said. "Rich people like the Coltons think their money can buy them everything they want. But after that mess they went through back in California, they should know the one thing it can't buy 'em is life. It can't buy your life, little girl. Nothing can."

So even if her dad paid him the ransom, Whitlaw had no intention of letting her live any more than he'd let her biological mother live.

Lakin tried to run faster. She knew she was literally running for her life.

Troy had been pushed back to the perimeter of the crime scene around the cabin now that the SAR team had finally arrived.

Kansas, her face pinched with the same fear Troy and Eli were feeling, led one of the dogs to the door of Lakin's cabin. It sniffed at the boards on the porch and then the door. As it sniffed the floor, it whined and backed off.

"The scent of chloroform might be lingering yet," a man with dark blond hair called out to Kansas. "I'm sure that's what was on the handkerchief."

So was Troy, and he had never smelled chloroform before. He just knew it was something used to make people lose consciousness. That was probably the only way the kidnapper would have gotten Lakin out of the cabin without a fight.

Troy didn't really believe people had stopped bullying her just because of her family and his. It was because Lakin had gotten stronger; she'd learned to fight back. She would have done that today if she'd been able.

But the chloroform would have made her as helpless as he'd been after falling off the oil rig. At least he'd had his coworkers around to jump in and save him. Lakin had no one.

They'd waited so damn long for search and rescue to show up, or so it had seemed, that the scent of the trail to her might have gone cold. She could be many miles away by now. And waiting around had only increased those miles.

But then the dog started barking and pulling Kansas across the front porch toward the woods. "He's got a scent!" Kansas yelled, and her face didn't look quite as pinched. She was hopeful.

Eli had been on the phone coordinating with the surveillance team setting up at his parents' for the kidnapper's follow-up call, but he hung up and started after Kansas.

Troy had overheard the ABI lieutenant earlier telling Kansas about the ransom request.

"Every kidnapper has to know that the person will want proof of life before turning over any money," Kansas had said. "That's good. That means she's alive."

Troy wanted to believe that, too, so badly. But he was too damn scared to think rationally at all. He waited just until Eli rushed into the woods after the SAR team before he ducked under the crime-scene tape and started after them.

The crime tech who'd identified the chloroform saw him but looked away, letting him go. He must have noticed how upset Troy was, how determined he was to find the woman he loved. And the guy hadn't just looked away from Troy—he'd looked off in the direction Kansas had gone. Maybe he understood what Troy was feeling because he cared about someone like that, too.

Troy stayed back a bit from the team, so that the officers and the dogs didn't notice him like the tech had. He didn't want to get in the way or cause a distraction. He didn't want to detract in any way from the search for Lakin. He just wanted to help.

And he wanted to be there when she was found.

She had to be found. Alive.

\* \* \*

Will held onto his wife's trembling body, trying to comfort her while seeking comfort himself. He was so damn scared. They'd gotten together a lot of money. Sasha's pottery business was doing well, and Will still had a lot of investments from selling the real estate business in California that he and his brother had inherited after losing the rest of their family. His brother, Ryan, who loved Lakin like she was his own daughter, had chipped in some of his inheritance investments, too.

Everybody wanted to get their girl safely back where she belonged: with them.

"Why hasn't he called yet?" Sasha asked, her voice muffled as her face was buried in his throat. Her tears wet his skin.

"He'll call back," Will said. "He has to call back…" If he wanted the money.

But was this really about money? Or was there another reason Lakin had been abducted?

Did her kidnapper really have any intention of letting her go?

# Chapter 23

Whatever Whitlaw had drugged her with back at the cabin was still affecting Lakin, slowing her down so that she felt as if she was running in quicksand. The slope was getting more treacherous with rocks and loose leaves making her slip and fall. Her hands were scraped.

But she didn't notice the pain or the blood seeping from her scratches. She clawed at branches, using them to pull herself up. She couldn't go back...

He was right behind her. Branches rustled, twigs snapped, and every now and then he coughed or cursed.

She waited for gunfire, like how he'd shot at Troy the other night. But none came. Maybe Whitlaw didn't want anyone to hear and figure out where they were.

How close to RTA were they?

Why hadn't she gone on some of the damn adventures herself? She hadn't wanted to run all over the mountain like she was now. If only she knew the area more, like her siblings and cousins. Hell, even

Mitch the lawyer had gone on more adventures than she had.

"You can run, girlie, but you can't hide," Whitlaw called out to her. He chuckled, but he sounded out of breath.

She was, too, her lungs burning from the altitude. She was going so slow, struggling so hard to fight the dizziness that kept threatening to overwhelm her.

As out of breath as he sounded, he also sounded close. Much too close.

She pushed her way through branches as the ground leveled out for a moment. And then…nothing was ahead of her or underneath her.

She dropped through the air, falling, falling…

Branches scratched at her hair and her clothes until finally she struck the ground.

Hard.

Pain radiated throughout her body and her head. And like at the cabin, blackness suddenly claimed her, pulling her deep into oblivion.

Troy continued to follow the sounds of dogs barking and the SAR team members talking back and forth. He recognized Kansas and Eli's voices and knew he had to hang back. If they saw him, they might have someone escort him back to the cabin. But he wanted to get close enough to clearly hear what they were saying. The dogs had to be following the scent still, but where?

"Tire tracks…"

"There's a truck…"

A vehicle was involved then. If a truck was still here, hopefully Lakin was, too. But where?

"And a cave…"

The dogs started barking louder, drowning out the voices. While Troy couldn't hear everything, he suspected he would have heard something over the barking if they'd found Lakin and her kidnapper. Gunfire or screaming maybe…

But there was just barking. So the cave was empty. Since the truck was still here, they couldn't have gotten anywhere fast. They had to be running around the woods. Maybe the kidnapper was trying to find a new place to hide Lakin and himself.

Or maybe Lakin, strong and resourceful, had managed to escape. Maybe the kidnapper was trying to find her.

Either Troy or the SAR team would have stumbled across them if they'd been going down the mountain, so they must've headed up. So he did, too.

Using the branches for balance, he pushed up the steep rocky incline. In one tree, he noticed a strand of long dark hair caught on a twig. Lakin had gone this way.

He wanted to call out to her, but if the kidnapper was looking for her, Troy didn't want to alert him to her whereabouts or to his. The last time Troy had tried to rescue her, he'd gotten shot at. He needed to be careful. He couldn't help Lakin if something happened to him. He was damn lucky that last time he'd only gotten a scratch on his face instead of a bullet in his brain. So he kept his head down and moved as quietly as he could through the trees, climbing up the rocks.

The dogs were not moving quietly. They barked loudly as they crashed through trees. He heard shouting again, in another direction.

He'd gone the wrong way, apparently.

But then he found another strand of hair on a branch. As he reached for it, his foot slipped. He dropped down hard on his butt, jarring his back as he hit the ground. His foot dangled over a steep drop.

Ignoring the twinge of pain in his back, he scooted closer to the edge and peered down into a deep ravine filled with trees and boulders. He looked at the branch above him, with that long strand of silky dark hair dangling from it.

The pain in his back moved to his heart. Had she fallen in the ravine?

"Lakin!" he yelled. He didn't care now who else heard him as long as she did. As long as she answered him. "Lakin!"

As long as she *could* answer him.

He could see where something, or *someone*, had broken branches in the ravine below. She had to be down there. Unable to answer him.

So he had to figure out how to reach her without falling himself.

Troy ducked under the branches of the trees that grew on the edge of the ravine, obscuring it so much that it was easy for someone to fall into it. With the edge of the bank eroding under those trees, one had fallen, giving him a gangplank to the bottom. But with branches sticking up from it, he couldn't walk down it. So he climbed down its branches, scratching his hands and his face. He didn't care. He didn't care about anything but finding Lakin.

The tree branches thinned toward the bottom of the ravine, snapping beneath his weight, and he dropped down into weeds and rocks beneath it.

Pain shot up his spine as his knee jammed into a rock. He flinched but willed the pain away. He had to find the woman he loved. He'd wasted so much time that they could have been together. He should have been living with her in the present instead of planning and saving for a future that might never come. If he couldn't find her…

He had to find her.

His throat raw from yelling, he shouted again, "Lakin!"

Pushing his way through the weeds at the bottom of the ravine, he found her lying in crushed ferns.

Blood dampened her hair from a wound on her head, and her eyes were closed. Was she just unconscious or…?

"Lakin!" he yelled.

But she didn't move at all. He couldn't even tell if she was breathing.

"Help!" he shouted, hurling the word toward the mouth of the ravine. "Help me!"

He could hear the dogs and the voices of the SAR team, but they sounded as if they were moving away from him, not toward him.

He stood up and shouted again. "Help! Come help! I found her!"

But had he found her too late?

Eli heard Troy shouting. But he was staring into the barrel of a gun that the man from Lakin's photograph pointed at him.

Whitlaw was older now, with several lines in his face. The same jagged scar trailed down one side of it. And his mouth was twisted into the same cruel sneer.

"It's too late," Whitlaw said.

"It is too late," Eli agreed. He held a gun, too, pointed directly at Whitlaw who stood a few yards up the mountain from him. Behind Eli were a couple of the SAR team members, holding back the dogs that Whitlaw had already threatened to shoot. Eli heard another gun cocking. Probably Kansas. His cousin would not let this man take him out. "Throw down your weapon. There's no way out of this, Whitlaw."

"It's too late for her," the older man said.

Eli heard the panic and desperation in Troy's hoarse voice as he continued shouting. The man was too proud to ask for help for himself. He needed help for Lakin.

"What did you do to her?" Kansas asked, moving closer to Eli.

Whitlaw chuckled. "Not a damn thing. She's the one who hurt herself. She ran right off the mountain."

Kansas gasped.

Fear gripped Eli, but he didn't lower his weapon. He didn't trust this man for a moment. If they got distracted, Whitlaw was going to shoot one of them. And with his obvious resentment of the Coltons, it was going to be either Eli or Kansas.

He had to take this guy out. Now. Without anyone else getting hurt.

But Eli couldn't stop thinking about Lakin hurt and needing his help.

# *Chapter 24*

Shouting pulled at Lakin in the darkness. Was Whitlaw yelling at her mother in her nightmare? Her mother was crying. Lakin was crying.

Or were the shouts from the man she loved? Troy?

"Help! I found her!"

It was him. She hoped.

Whitlaw couldn't find her, or he would kill her for certain, just like he'd killed her mother. That thought was so unbearable, like the pain, that she slipped back into oblivion. But not into the nightmare.

Instead she dreamed of Troy, of their first dance, of their first kiss. Of all of their kisses.

She'd loved him for so long.

"Come back to me," his deep voice, gruff with emotion, pleaded. "Come back to me…"

Where was she? She couldn't tell. Couldn't see beyond the darkness.

"I love you…"

The words pulled at her more than the shouting.

"I love you," he repeated, his voice cracking. "Please come back to me…"

Where was she? Was she dead? But she could feel. Her love for him and the pain. It pounded so hard inside her head, reverberating off her skull. She flinched from the intensity of it. But she didn't want to leave him.

Not Troy.

She fought her way from the blackness, opening her eyes. She squinted against the light and the pain. Why so much pain?

"What happened?" she asked in a whisper. Her throat was raw, and her voice muffled by the mask over her mouth. It wasn't the tape or the handkerchief. It was plastic and full of oxygen.

The grasp on her hand tightened, and she peered up to find Troy leaning over one side of her while a stranger sat on the other. Wherever they were, they were moving, bouncing along a road. Sirens blared, making her flinch again. The pain intensified so much that she couldn't hang on.

She had to let go of Troy.

Had to let go of the pain.

Of consciousness.

Ignoring the pain in his back and his knee, Troy paced the waiting room. "How long does it take to do a CT?" he asked Eli.

Leaning against a wall, Eli shook his head. "I don't know. They need to make sure there's no bleeding or swelling on her brain."

Troy flinched at the thought. "She regained consciousness in the ambulance," he reminded her brother. "She asked what happened."

Was that a good thing or a bad thing, though? Didn't she remember what had happened, that Whitlaw had abducted her? Or was it the fall she'd forgotten?

She'd gotten hurt because of that horrible man. He was in custody now; he couldn't hurt her.

But a brain injury could. Even though she'd regained consciousness, the bleeding or swelling could still take her life. Troy knew that many people, even movie stars and celebrities, had lost their lives because of traumatic brain injuries like that.

His breath caught in his lungs with the panic pressing on his chest. For a second, he couldn't move.

Eli reached out and grasped his shoulder. "She'll be all right. She regained consciousness. My little sister is tough. She'll be fine."

Troy wasn't sure if her older brother was trying to convince him or himself. "Lakin is tough," he agreed.

She'd gotten away from that creep. And she'd put up with Troy for years, with the long-distance relationship so many other people, besides Billy Hoover and Eric Seller, must have pointed out to her was going nowhere. Troy had been such an idiot.

"You're an idiot!" Kansas exclaimed.

Troy jerked his head toward the door to the waiting room, expecting to see Kansas pointing at him. But she was talking to another man. Troy had seen him around enough to know that he was Eli's partner with ABI. Asher or something like that.

Eli groaned and levered himself away from the wall as if he needed to break up the fight. But then the tech with the dark blond hair stepped between the two of them.

"Ah, Scott Montgomery to the rescue," Eli remarked.

Unlike Asher who'd obviously upset her, Scott spoke softly to Kansas. She offered him a faint smile before glowering at Asher again.

Troy focused on them for a moment, mostly so he would stop worrying about Lakin and how badly she might be injured. "What's the deal with all that?" he asked Eli.

"I think both my partner and the brilliant tech have crushes on my beautiful cousin," Eli said with a chuckle that sounded almost pitying. "But Kansas is too focused on finding the serial killer to give either of them the time of day."

It was true; Kansas walked away from both men and headed toward Troy and Eli. "What have you heard? How is she?" she demanded.

"Nothing new yet," Troy said.

"Uncle Will and Aunt Sasha were pulling into the lot as I was walking into the lobby," Kansas warned Eli. "They're going to want news."

"We all want news," Troy said. The longer it took for this damn CT scan, the more worried he got. What was taking so long? Had they found the very things they were worried about? Bleeding, swelling… Was she going to be okay?

If only he'd found her sooner…

Once he had, it hadn't taken the SAR team long to get them up from the ravine and down the mountain to the ambulance. Hopefully they'd gotten her medical attention fast enough. He couldn't consider the alternative.

He couldn't consider losing her.

But even if she recovered, he might still lose her. He'd been the idiot that Kansas had called Eli's partner. Troy had been waiting for his future to start instead of living it. Instead of just focusing on his love for Lakin and not worrying about anything else.

Now, he was worried only about her.

Ever since he got the ransom call, Will had been scared to death that they might lose their daughter. He'd held onto the hope that if he paid the ransom, they would get her back. Or that Eli and Kansas would find her.

But Troy Amos had.

Eli had told them when he'd called them. Troy had found Lakin, and they were in an ambulance on their way to the hospital.

"Why?" Will had managed to choke out.

Eli knew better than to sugarcoat things with him. He'd replied honestly, "She was running to escape her kidnapper and fell."

Will hadn't asked any more questions. Maybe because he hadn't wanted to know how badly she was hurt. He just wanted to see his daughter.

So did Sasha. Together, they rushed into the hospital waiting room, holding onto each other.

"How is she?" Will asked his son who stood next to Troy and Kansas.

"We're waiting for them to come back from CT and let us know," Eli replied.

"CT?" Sasha whispered. "She hit her head?"

His face grim, Eli nodded.

"She regained consciousness in the ambulance," Troy said, his voice gruff.

"She'll be fine, Uncle Will. Aunt Sasha, she'll be fine," Kansas said, but she sounded as desperate to believe that as they were.

"Lakin's strong," Eli said.

Will knew that, but he still remembered the sweet little toddler who'd woken up with nightmares so often after she came to live with them. She wasn't the only one who had nightmares back then. He and Eli had had some, too, after finding the bodies of his parents and Caroline and her killer.

But Lakin was alive. And she would stay that way. She had to…

Will couldn't lose anyone else he loved.

"Sir," Troy said. Tears shimmered in his green eyes. "May I speak to you and Mrs. Colton for a moment…alone…?"

Troy had found her; he'd ridden with her in the

ambulance. Maybe he knew more than the others. Will was almost afraid to talk to him.

But Sasha, probably knowing that Troy needed comfort as much as they did, released Will to hug their daughter's longtime boyfriend. "Thank you for finding her, Troy," she said, tears streaming down her face.

Troy deserved their gratitude, let alone some of their time. So Will walked with the young man and Sasha toward a quiet corner of the waiting room that was beginning to fill up with Coltons and Amoses.

So many people loved Lakin, but no one more than Troy. She had to be okay for his sake as much as for hers and theirs. She had to be okay.

# Chapter 25

Lakin heard voices, but these were soft whispers, not the shouts from her nightmares or even from earlier… Was it today that she'd heard Troy yelling for help? How much time had passed since she'd slipped and fallen trying to escape from Whitlaw? From her biological mother's murderer?

She gasped at the sharp jab of pain over the loss. The woman had given Lakin life and had done her best to protect that life.

"She's awake," a soft voice said with awe. "Sweetheart, are you all right?"

And she opened her eyes to the mother she knew, the one who'd been there for her as long as she could remember. Who'd loved and supported her unconditionally. "Mom…" Lakin whispered, her throat raspy.

Then she saw her dad leaning over her mother and her brothers and even Hetty and Mrs. Amos and a couple of the other Amos siblings.

Where was Troy?

She didn't see him even though she looked around for him. He was tall; she should have been able to see him over the others. But instead of asking for him, she forced a smile for all the worried faces staring back at her. "I thought there's a limit on the number of visitors a person can have."

She knew she was in the hospital. An IV line was taped into a vein in her arm, and she lay partially inclined in a bed with railings.

"There are too many of us Coltons and Amoses for them to hold us to that limit," her father said with a grin, but his eyes were damp like her mom's.

"I think we can break this one law," Eli said, his voice gruff.

Lakin shook her head and flinched at a jolt of pain near the base of her skull. "No more law breaking," she murmured. "I'm okay…"

Or she would be when she saw Troy. Where was he? Why wasn't he with her?

"That's all we wanted to know," Mrs. Amos said, "that you would be all right, sweet girl."

Lakin smiled at the beautiful woman she'd hoped would one day be her mother-in-law. But Troy wasn't ready to make a commitment obviously. He wasn't even here for her.

Although he'd been in the ambulance. Had something happened to him? She wanted to ask about him, but first she had to know…

"Did you catch Whitlaw?" she asked her brother.

Eli nodded.

"He killed my birth mother," she said. "He told me so when he was chasing me. He would have killed me, too, back then if she hadn't left me in that grocery store."

"We knew you were loved before we loved you," her adoptive mother said, tears shimmering in her blue eyes. "And now we know how much."

Her birth mother had loved her.

"Eli and I need to talk to Whitlaw," Kansas said and jerked her head toward the door. "We can go now that we know you're all right."

Lakin hugged them both goodbye. She was all right physically. Emotionally she was still a mess, especially because Troy wasn't here.

But when Eli and Kansas opened the door, he was standing there out in the hall.

Had he just gotten here? Or had he been out there the whole time? Afraid to see her? Afraid that she might not want him here like he hadn't wanted her at his bedside all those weeks ago?

Everybody else followed Eli and Kansas's lead, hugging and kissing her before walking out into the hall.

While everyone else was walking out, Troy stepped inside the room. He was limping again, and a grimace crossed his face as he moved around the room until he was beside her bed. Finally the door shut behind her last visitor, leaving them alone together.

Lakin stared at Troy for a long while. She felt caught in his green-eyed gaze, her image reflecting

back at her. She was bruised and scraped up with a
bandage on the back of her head.

He was bruised and scraped up, too, his clothes
torn.

"What happened to you?" she asked.

His breath caught for a second, then released in
a ragged sigh. "I went into that ravine to find you."

She wasn't sure it was a ravine she'd fallen into
or if she'd just gone off the side of the mountain.
She'd accidentally gone over; he'd purposely risked
his life for hers.

"You hurt your back again," she said, tears rushing
to her eyes for the pain he had to be feeling.

He shook his head. "Whacked my knee on a rock,"
he said. "It's bruised but not broken. They think my
back will be fine."

"Good," she said. And then she had to ask, "Does
that mean you're going to go back to the oil rigs?"

Was he going to leave her again?

"I'm sorry," he said, his voice heavy with emotion.

As her heart broke, she closed her eyes. "Then…
just go…" she choked out. She couldn't keep doing
this; she couldn't keep saying goodbye to the man
she loved and not know if he was going to be able to
make it back to her.

Troy's heart broke from the tears sliding down her
face. "I'm so sorry," he said, and he pushed down
one railing so he could sit on the bed and pull her
into his arms.

But her body was stiff with rejection. "If you're going to leave again, just go," she said. "I can't keep saying goodbye to you."

"I'm not leaving," he said.

Finally she opened her eyes, wet with tears. "What?"

"I'm never leaving you again," he said. "I'm sorry I was so stubborn and stupid to think that money mattered when the only thing that matters is love. No, the only thing that matters is you. I love you so much, Lakin, and I'm so sorry. Can you ever forgive me for putting off our future, for worrying about things that don't really matter?"

"I thought they mattered, too," she said. "I thought we needed more money saved before we bought our business."

"But you did it anyway," he said with a smile of pride at her bravery. "When the opportunity came up, you took it. Just like you must have to get away from Whitlaw."

She shuddered and clutched him closer. "I was so scared."

"Me, too," he admitted. "I've never been so scared. Not even when I fell off that oil rig. And I realized when you were missing that nothing else matters but us being together. I was just so scared of being a burden to you."

She pressed her fingers over his lips. "I love you. No matter what. Sickness and health."

"Will you say those words to me?"

"I just did," she said, her forehead furrowing a bit.

"I would drop down to one knee, but it would be a little hard right now," he said. "What I'm asking, Lakin Colton, is for you to be my wife, my partner in business and life. I love you so much, and I will do my best to spend the rest of our lives making up for the time we've been apart while I've been stupid."

She chuckled and pressed her fingers to his lips again. "You've been stubborn," she agreed. "But you're not stupid. I know your family struggled after your dad died, and you worry about security."

"You're my security," he said. "You're my home. You're my everything. I asked your dad and mom for their permission to marry you. They said it's up to you. Maybe they think I've already blown my chance. Have I, Lakin? Have I waited too long to start our future?"

She shook her head. "No, our future starts now. Yes, I will marry you. I will be your partner in all things. I love you so very much, Troy Amos."

Finally she'd said the words back to him again. He had her love back. He had Lakin back.

"And I love you." He lowered his head and kissed her lips. All the pain he'd ever felt disappeared; he felt only love and gratitude that she was safe and she was his as much as he was hers.

Kansas was irritated with Asher. He'd wanted to start the interrogation of Jasper Whitlaw without her and Eli. Sure, he figured they wanted to be there for

Lakin, and he wasn't wrong about that. Even Scott had pointed that out. But he could have just waited; it was as if he hadn't believed that Lakin was going to be okay.

Kansas hadn't wanted to consider the possibility. Anyway, Lakin was fine. And from what Mom and Dad had insinuated when they all left her and Troy alone together, she was probably engaged by now.

Which for some reason made Kansas even more determined to find the Fiancée Killer. There was no proof yet that any of his victims had actually been engaged, though. The ones they'd identified had been single.

Except for Mrs. Whitlaw; Stella, who was undoubtedly Lakin's biological mom, had been a married woman. But she was dead, and her husband had confessed to killing her.

Facing Jasper Whitlaw, Kansas began, "We have you on your wife's murder as well as the abduction of Lakin Colton, kidnapping, extortion and the attempted murder of Troy Amos. You have a long list of charges being brought against you. So tell us about the other women."

"Other women?" Whitlaw asked. "Stella was the tramp. Cheated on me when I was prison and gave birth to that little whiny brat."

"Lakin was never whiny," Eli defended his sister. "She was always as sweet and kind as she is now."

Whitlaw snorted. "People thought the same about her mother, wondered why Stella was with me. She probably thought she could save me or reform me, but in the end nobody was able to save her."

"Why'd you come after Lakin?" Eli asked.

Whitlaw shrugged. "Figured she might remember what happened, and I didn't want to go to back to prison."

"She was there when you killed her mother?"

He sighed. "Stella didn't die right away. She managed to get the kid to the grocery store. But she died shortly after that."

"From the beating you gave her," Eli said. "Lakin used to wake up with nightmares."

"And she didn't like shouting," Kansas remembered. "But what about the other women?"

"What other women?" Whitlaw sounded annoyed now. "I only grabbed Lakin because I figured it wasn't fair. She got the cushy life as a Colton. I was owed some of that money, too."

"You were owed nothing," Eli said. "But you owe plenty to other people. Closure. The truth."

"I don't know if Stella's body was ever found," he said. "That's up to you to figure out."

"What about the other women?" Kansas persisted.

"I haven't killed any other women," Whitlaw said. He leaned back and shook his head. "I'm no freaky serial killer if that's what you're trying to pin on me. Hell, give me the dates, and I'm sure I've got alibis."

Kansas figured he probably did. He wasn't the killer they were looking for.

She and Eli left him alone in the interrogation room and stepped into the hall.

"It's not him," Asher said as he walked up to join them.

Of course he would have already figured that out.

"I checked the dates of the other abductions, and he was on his parole officer's radar then. He was regularly checking in with him and wasn't anywhere near this vicinity until a few weeks ago," Asher continued.

Eli sighed. "Did you check out Billy Hoover and Eric Seller too?"

"Billy Hoover and Eric Seller?" Kansas repeated. "Why would you check out Billy? And isn't Seller a RTA client?"

"Troy came up with some other possible suspects when someone was stalking Lakin," Eli said.

"Maybe we should give him a job," Asher said.

But Kansas suspected Troy would have one with Lakin soon. She'd heard about the old Shelby Hotel.

"I already checked out Billy and Eric," Eli said. "Both have alibis for the dates the other women were killed. Bobby Reynolds actually was the alibi for Billy. He locked him up for drunk driving."

Kansas nearly growled with frustration. "We have to find this killer…"

Before he killed again. She had no doubt that he would keep killing until he was caught.

## *Chapter 26*

Lakin stepped back and stared at the two-story building. Pride and gratitude overwhelmed her. Gone was the weathered wood siding that had been rotted in places. In just the few weeks since she'd been kidnapped, she and Troy had replaced it with warm, cream-colored siding and rich burgundy trim. Troy had even handcrafted a new sign for out front: Suite Home. He'd made another for the two suites inside that they would eventually combine into their private residence: Sweet Home.

He wrapped his arm around her shoulders and hugged her to his side. "Do you like it?" he asked.

She shook her head. "No. I love it." Then she slid her arm around his waist and stretched up on tiptoe to kiss his jaw. "I love you."

He'd worked so hard on the renovations that she'd been worried he was going to reinjure his back, but while he limped from time to time, he was doing well. Even though his health wasn't as big a concern as it had been, she knew he was still worried about money. Her business loan had been approved, and she'd paid her father back. But until the hotel was completely up and running again, they would struggle to make ends meet.

But just like the bank that granted them the loan, she had faith in their business plan and in their future. There was nothing the two of them couldn't do together, especially after they'd individually survived what could have been fatal falls.

Troy turned his head and lowered his mouth to hers, kissing her deeply, passionately. He pulled back a bit, panting for breath, and whispered, "I love you, too, partner." He lowered his head and kissed her again.

"Get a room!" a deep voice scoffed.

Laughing, Lakin stepped back from Troy and turned to find her brother Mitch standing behind them. "We already have a few ready for guests," she said. They were counting on the money from those for the loan payments and the renovations necessary to get more rooms ready. "We'll have twenty-four in total."

"It looks great, guys," Mitch praised them.

Pride suffused Lakin again. Her brothers were all so successful that praise from one of them meant a lot to her. "Thanks." She pulled away from Troy to hug him.

"You have more to thank me for than a compliment," Mitch said. He turned to Troy. "Your former employer settled the suit."

Troy released a shaky breath. "Really?"

Mitch nodded. "For even more than we were asking."

Troy's green eyes widened with surprise. "Really?" he repeated.

"And they didn't just give you a settlement," Mitch said. "Your mom will get one, too."

Troy's long body shook slightly, and tears glistened in his green eyes. "Oh my God, that's great. Thank you." He hugged her brother.

Mitch patted his back. "More important, they're going to up their safety protocols. The suggestions you made are already being put into practice."

Troy trembled again. "That's good."

But Lakin saw the sadness cross his handsome face, and she knew what he was thinking. It was too late for his dad, even for himself, to not suffer an injury. "That will help others," Lakin said. "That's so good, Troy."

He smiled at her and nodded. "Yeah, it is. Hopefully nobody else will lose someone they love."

Not on the oil rigs. But Lakin was still worried that with a serial killer on the loose, more lives would be lost. Eli and Kansas were working hard to find that person, though. And she had faith in her family, just as she had faith in her and Troy's future. Even more so now.

"Come on, take a look at the place," Lakin urged Mitch.

As they were showing him around inside, someone knocked on the front door and opened it.

"Hello there? Are you open for business yet?" Eric Seller called out.

Troy tensed.

"Remember that Eli and Kansas ruled him out," Lakin whispered to her fiancé. She turned to greet the man. "We have a few suites ready."

The man glanced at her hand and pointed at the ring. Then he clasped Troy's shoulder. "Good job," he said. "Congratulations on the hotel and the engagement."

Troy must have heard the sincerity that Lakin heard because he relaxed and grinned at Eric. "Thank you."

"You two inspired me to look up my old high school sweetheart," he said. "I spent all the years since graduation kicking myself for not trying long distance when we went away for college. I reached out to her and found out that she's never married, either. We've been talking online and on the phone and have been looking for a place to meet in person. I'd like to book a couple of your suites for that meeting."

"Congratulations to you," Lakin said. "I'm so happy that you reached out to her."

He nodded. "Like I said, you two inspired me. I think that's why I was so invested in you getting engaged."

"We'll be getting married soon, too," Troy said. "Just want to get our hotel ready so guests will have a place to stay."

"Brilliant," Eric said. "I think you'll do well here. If you need any investors, let me know."

Troy and Mitch exchanged a grin, and Troy replied, "No, we're going to be just fine."

Lakin grinned, too. "We're going to be better than fine." They were going to be happy because all their dreams were going to come true.

Troy could have kicked himself for all the years he'd worried about money, about making it, about not having enough of it. Finally, when he'd stopped worrying about it, he had it. The irony was not lost on him. After Mitch and Seller left the hotel, he laughed and shook his head.

"What's funny?" Lakin asked.

"Not funny really," Troy admitted. "Just sad that I've been such an idiot, worrying about all the wrong things."

She smiled. "Money?"

He nodded. "I'm very sorry for what I've put you through. And my mother…"

"She got a settlement, too," Lakin said. "You won't have to worry about her, either."

"According to her, I didn't ever have to worry about her," Troy admitted. "She's already tried to give me back the money I've given her. I have a feeling we're going to get a pretty big wedding gift from her."

"Wedding," Lakin said, and her face lit up with a beautiful smile. "I can't wait."

"Me, neither," Troy said. "I can't wait to be your husband. To start our family." Emotion overwhelmed him just thinking about their future and how wonderful it was going to be.

Lakin grabbed his hand and tugged him toward the hall with the finished suites. "Maybe we can put in some practice for starting that family," she said, turning back to wink at him.

His pulse quickened with desire. He loved her so much, and yet he would never be able to make love with her enough, to express all his love for her. But he intended to try.

He swung her up in his arms and carried her over the threshold into the suite they'd had so much fun renovating together. Then he laid her on the bed and followed her down.

They both wriggled out of their clothes until skin slid over skin. He made love to her slowly, with his hands and with his mouth, caressing and kissing every inch of her. Finally he slid inside her, joining their bodies like their souls were already joined. And he thrust in and out, in and out, until she clutched him with her arms and legs and her inner muscles. Then her body shuddered, and she screamed his name as she found her release.

And he found his, the pleasure so intense it was almost painful.

Panting for breath, he levered himself up so he wouldn't crush her and leaned his forehead against hers. "You know what they say, practice makes perfect."

"You're already perfect," she told him.

"You are."

"We're perfect for each other."

And they were; they had always been and always would be.

Parker had texted Lakin a while ago about something he needed to find in the RTA office, but she must have been busy at the hotel. It took a while before she texted him back.

When she did text him again, she added, Call Genna McDougal and offer her my old job.

Her old job. Parker felt a pang of loss. He missed Lakin, and not just because she knew where everything was and how to do everything. He missed seeing his sister every day.

And then he felt another pang at her proposed replacement, aka the bane of his existence. But he couldn't tell Lakin that or he would have to tell her what had happened between them...

\* \* \* \* \*